I Bought
Monk's Ferrari

I Bought the Monk's Ferrari

Ravi Subramanian

Rupa . Co

First Published 2007
Nineth Impression 2011

Published by
Rupa Publications India Pvt. Ltd.
7/16, Ansari Road, Daryaganj,
New Delhi 110 002

Sales Centres:

Allahabad Bengaluru Chennai
Hyderabad Jaipur Kathmandu
Kolkata Mumbai

Mindways Design
1410 Chiranjiv Tower
43 Nehru Place
New Delhi 110 019

Printed in India by
Rekha Printers Pvt. Ltd.
A-102/1, Okhla Industrial Area, Phase-II
New Delhi-110 020

Dedicated to all those:

Who are not astronauts, but reach out to the stars
Who are not pole vaulters, but leap above the bars
Who are not in F1, but drive in the fast lane
and for whom anything but a Ferrari, will be a big shame.

Contents

What Is The Ferrari?

Acknowledgements

To the Fiat Motor Company, for the Ferrari they have created.

To my wife, Dharini, for all the compromises she made; her support, when I was writing this book will never fade from my memories.

To my daughter, Anusha, who is proud of me—the author, forgetting conveniently that I have better accomplishments as a banker.

To all the readers of my first book, which became a bestseller in the very first month of its release.

Thank you all.

Prologue

There was a young boy, who belonged to a typical middle-class family—which, like all other middle-class families, ran only on two wheels. His parents, a college professor and a school teacher, struggled to educate him and his brother. Even though they had to go beyond their means to do this, they did not compromise on quality. They gave their children the best they could with their limited means. The only time this young boy saw a four-wheeler was when he and his brother would furiously pedal to school, their bicycle wheels leaving behind a trail of dust. The first time he saw his parents progress in life was when his father bought a scooter when the boy was ten years old. But that was it. He aspired for a four-wheeler, which was never to be. He would see in magazines, movies and be taken in by the fancy cars that presented themselves in full gloss. As he grew up, a dream started brewing in him. He, who had pedalled a bicycle all his life, wanted more. And, when he decided to reach out for more, he aspired for the best. Not only did he aspire for a car, he aspired for the king of the cars ... the Ferrari.

Ferrari ... when most people come across this word, they think of two things—speed and sport. It is one of the most sought after cars in the automobile history. On the race circuit, it has set the track on fire, winning more races than any other car. Not only does it have a tough and furious demeanour, it is also as much a graceful and delicate car.

Since the first one came to existence around seven decades ago, Ferrari has been a panache incarnate—it defines not only Italian style, but global style, as well. Ferraris have been referred to as the ultimate status symbol, a rich man's toy, an answer to a mid-life crisis, a proof of piles of stock money—and if that was not enough, as the finest of cars in the world. Depending on whether one is speaking out of envy, disdain or admiration, a Ferrari is all of those and more. A Ferrari is not about individual spec sheet of an automobile. It is a dream.

As with all dreams, a Ferrari takes a while to come true. The assembly line produces a mere twenty-seven cars a day—a little over five thousand a year. With the exception of the engine, each one is handcrafted and is unique.

Ferrari founder, Enzo Ferrari (1898–1988), built the first car in 1940. However, it was not till after the Second World War that Ferrari started making cars bearing his name, founding today's Ferrari S.P.A. in 1945. However, the present Ferraris are more sleek and futuristic, compared to the past models. Over the last few decades, their price has raced ahead like the racing cars themselves, with the price being over $1,50,000 per car.

For the young boy, this racing car was a dream, an aspiration, his vision of success, and the awaited destination at the end of his long winding journey.

His dream car, Ferrari, took its real shape when he happened to glimpse it for the first time, from the aeroplane window, while embarking on his maiden journey in the pursuit of a career in Delhi. True, he was far, far away from the Ferrari but the sight of it only strengthened his resolve to ride in it.

The second sighting was when he chanced upon one from close quarters. He ogled at it, chased it, and then pledged to acquire it. He was within breathing distance of someone else's Ferrari and realised that this could be his, one day. The thought of owning a Ferrari, made him feel happy, feel elated, feel elevated. The dream could become a reality, after all.

And then he took a ride in a Ferrari. The first time he got behind the steering ... and felt the pulse, the exhilaration and the adrenalin ... he felt the Ferrari. That was when he realised that he could control the levers. The drivers which were required for him to successfully acquire a Ferrari were in his own hands.

It was entirely upon him to be successful, to be a winner. The Ferrari could be his if he did the right things required for it.

The first section of this book marks the beginning of his pilgrimage, during which he faced monstrous hurdles and adversities, but he learnt lessons that led him towards making his dream real. Then come the Ten Commandments, not from God to Moses, but from life itself to all those who dare to aspire. They are the traits and characteristics of all those who have earned their Ferrari and that which the readers need to imbibe and demonstrate to get closer to it. And, the last section of the book, details as to what a Ferrari actually is, and why it is so important for each and every individual to aspire for a Ferrari.

Enzo Ferrari had once said: *The greatest thing a race car driver could do, would be to die behind the wheels of my car.*

He could not have got closer to reality than this. Not only every sports car driver, but every individual in this world, wants to acquire the car that he built, the car with the prancing black horse in a yellow background on its boot. This car epitomises success, achievements, happiness and all that a person seeks in life.

Through this book, that young lad, i.e. me, shares with you his rendezvous with the Ferrari and the Ten Commandments he learnt in the process, which will in turn, guide the readers in their journey to the destination—the elusive Ferrari.

The Journey Begins

One

The Journey Begins

May 1993

'Passengers travelling to Delhi by IC 812 please pass through the security check and wait for your boarding call.'

When I heard this announcement on the public address system at the HAL Military Airport, Bangalore, I hastily put down the newspaper and stood up from my chair. A few drops of sweat broke onto my forehead. My hand instantaneously went into the front pocket of my trousers, pulled out a neat white handkerchief, and wiped the sweat off my brow.

> *You don't have to be great to start, but you have to start to be great.*
>
> ZIG ZIGLAR

Just about thirty minutes back, my mother and my

cousin Mani had dropped me at the airport. Now it seemed like ages since that had happened. I had not slept the whole of last night. I was anxious ... a touché, worried. I did not know what to expect.

Five days back, on last Friday, I was in a classroom, not too far from the airport, in Golden Enclave, a posh residential–commercial building. It was the last day of the month-long induction programme for the latest batch of MBAs at Tata-IBM. Naren Aiyer, the head of the PC division and Dick Richards, the training head for the company were in the room with thirty-one MBA passouts, who had newly joined the company.

'Friends, we have now come to our last session. I am sure that all of you are eager to know your postings.' There was pin-drop silence in the classroom. No one spoke. On the day they had come in for their induction, they had been asked for their location and functional preferences and everyone had given in their first three choices. Now on this fateful day, every soul in the room, was waiting to hear if he or she had been allotted the preferred location.

It was 1993 and IBM was returning to India after fifteen years of hibernation, after being thrown out of India along with the Coca Cola Company, by the Janata Government in 1978, because they refused to dilute their ownership of hundred percent of their subsidiaries in India. It was a coveted company and had got the 'Day One' position in all management institutions—a position, every MBA would know, is only given to the crème de la crème among the recruiters.

There were thirty-one freshers in that room, thrilled to have got an offer from IBM. All of them knew that irrespective of their posting allocations they would stick to the company.

Gajananam, bhuta ganathi sevitham,
Kapitha Jambuphala, sarabhashitham…

A small prayer escaped my lips. Secret prayers were being chanted by all, to their own private gods.… So, I prayed even harder.

Dick went on, 'Naren, will you please pass me the list?' The wait was unbearable.

'OK, here we go…'

All the anxious thirty-one faces eagerly leaned forward and rested the elbows on the desks in front. The backs of the seats were gloriously divorced from their occupants.

'Sridhar Rajagopal … AS/400 Product Team, Mumbai.'

'Priya Mathew, Sales, Mumbai …' and then another frustrating pause.

Dick stopped, pulled out his slim-framed glasses … they were, in fact, rimless spectacles … for the first time those minuscule ones made their presence felt in India and glanced at everyone in the room.

'I wanted to tell you all that in these allocations, we have given priority to the location preferences of women and to those who want to join the sales department.'

'Vijay Krishnan ... RS/6000, Delhi.'

He was sitting next to me.

'Shit!!!' Exclaimed Vijay. 'I am ... Sooo ... oorry,' he said out loud when he realised that everyone in the room including Dick and Naren were staring at him. He wanted to be in Bangalore.

'Mukul Mathur .... Delhi.'

'Sudarshan Chakravarthy ... Chennai, PC Sales.'

'Sapna Agarwal ... Training, Bangalore.'

'Ravi Subramanian ... System Sales, New Delhi.'

My heart sank. Dick went on for another ten minutes, but I did not hear a word.

I did not want to go to Delhi. The preferences I had given were, Chennai, Bangalore and Mumbai, in that order. And now, I would have to go to Delhi. Though I had relatives in the city, I had never stayed there and the metropolis scared me. But I did not have a choice.

This was how I ended up at the Bangalore airport, waiting for the boarding call for the Indian Airlines flight to Delhi. But why would anyone perspire the way I was? In the cool Bangalore weather, inside an air-conditioned airport, my shirt was almost drenched with sweat. I was going to a new city, an alien city, but that was not the reason. The reason was completely different and had no connection whatsoever with Delhi....

This was the first time I was going to travel by air. Yes, this was my first flight. I was excited and nervous. Worried, too. What if the aeroplane crashed? What if I felt dizzy at over thirty thousand feet above the ground? Earlier in the morning, after we had reached the airport, putting on a brave front I sent back my mom and cousin. But here I was, nervous like hell.

'Passengers travelling to Delhi are requested to complete their security check, identify their baggage and proceed toward the aircraft through Gate No. 2.' I ran towards the gate the moment I heard this. Unaware of how the process worked, I was apprehensive that in case I was late the flight might take off without me. However, I learnt only later, that once the boarding pass is issued, the flight normally does not take off without the passenger.

After the security check, I walked towards Gate No.2. It took me some time to find it, as I was not familiar with the airport. Walking out of the gate, as I approached the aircraft, I stood wonderstruck at the sight of the colossal machine before me. On its both sides, written in large fonts, was the name ...

Indian Airlines. I had always seen these aircraft in the sky. This was the first time I was seeing one from such close quarters.

I chanted a small prayer as I climbed up the iron stairs with a jeep beneath, something which people call a mechanical ladder.

As I stepped into the aircraft, a matronly lady greeted, 'Welcome to Indian Airlines,' and I smiled back. My chest swelled with pride. I was entering an aeroplane for the first time in my life! No one from my family had even ventured close to an airport, leave alone travelling by air.

Ahead of me, I saw two rows of seats with a passage in between. I was thoroughly baffled.

'May I help you?' The lost look on my face was too obvious, and it made an air hostess come to my rescue. She took the boarding pass from my hand, glanced at it and said, 'Seventeen Alpha ... sensing my blank look she continued, Seventeen A, Sir ... further down, on your right.' I walked down the aisle and ultimately found the seat. It was a window seat. In fact, all seats with suffix 'A' are window seats in all aircraft, but I did not know it then. I hadn't asked at the check-in counter for it would make my ignorance too obvious.

I took my seat and belted myself ... then carefully watched all the instructions and demonstrations given by the air hostess. Everything was new to me, so much so that when the air hostess said that in case of an emergency landing on water the seat cushions can be used as a flotation device, my hands automatically went below the seat trying to figure out as to how the seat could be removed and used. When I could not figure it out, I raised my hand to ask for a clarification. No one noticed. Embarrassed, I pulled my hand down. The demonstration ended, the equipments were carted off to the overhead bins, the air hostess disappeared somewhere ... where? I had no clue. It took me a good fifty minutes to realise that all you are required to do is to press the button above your head, and someone would attend to you. If only I knew....

The aircraft taxied on the runway and stopped. A minute later, it started jogging, then galloping, then sprinting till it finally flew. I looked out the window like a small child as the ground ran in the opposite direction and slowly as it went into a free fall below the aircraft. As the flight started gaining altitude, before large buildings started turning into small insect-like objects and everything on the ground started fading away...something caught my attention.

Cruising on the road below, fading fast from my vision, leaving a puff of dust as it sped on an early morning empty highway, shining exquisitely in the morning sun was a bright red car ... then the plane hit a cloud ... a thick cloud and everything disappeared from my sight. A mammoth, thick white blanket stood between the plane and the earth below … between me and the immaculate, bright red **FERRARI.**

My flight of life had begun.… And, it was some kind of a divine intervention that just as the aircraft soared above the clouds, for an instant, I caught the glimpse of a Ferrari.… A car I had always dreamt of, I had aspired for, I had promised myself to own one day.

I was twenty-three then, and a month out of IIM-Bangalore.

Two

The Sighting

May 2006

The flight from Rio landed at Chhatrapati Shivaji International Airport, Mumbai, at midnight. A twenty-four hours' journey, intermeshed with an excruciating wait at the Paris airport, had taken its toll on me. I was exhausted, wanting desperately to reach home and hit my bed.

> *Reach high, for stars lie*
> *hidden in your soul.*
> *Dream deep, for every dream*
> *precedes the goal.*
> RALPH VAULL STARR

When I reached the immigration-queue my heart sank. Ahead of me was an ocean of humanity, awaiting their turn. Will things ever improve in this country?, I thought hopelessly and joined the queue. I didn't have a choice. I pulled out my mobile phone to call home and tell Dharini, my wife, that my flight had landed. But my phone went dead. I tried switching it on and it defiantly refused to show the slightest of response to my futile efforts. The battery was dead—an obvious outcome of the innumerable games that kept me occupied during my long journey.

Somehow the queue managed to move and I crossed the immigration check and then made my way to the conveyor belt area. As luck would have it, my baggage was the last to appear on the rail. I collected my bags and walked out of the airport. Hundreds of drivers stood there, holding large boards with names of passengers they had come to pick up, half of them were wrongly spelt, I could tell even without knowing their correct names. Had an attempt been made to lay down all the placards side by side on the ground, they would cover an entire football field.

My miserable luck continued. I could not find any placard bearing my name. Those who travel regularly would be aware that these days the travel agents SMS the driver's contact number to the passenger. This helps to trace the driver.

However, that was of no use on this fateful day. Anything that could go wrong, was going wrong. A phone charging booth I spotted, already had four or five people crowding around it.

I considered, albeit for a fleeting moment, the thought of waiting there but eventually discarded it.

I cursed my secretary under my breath and walked back to a phone booth hoping to call her and ask as to where my pick-up was. Maybe, it was not her fault after all. How could she be held responsible if the cab does not turn up! I changed my mind and walked back to the exit point looking around with the hope that I might have missed the placard with my name, but I could not see one.

Dharini had offered to hold back our driver and send the car, but I did not want to pay him overtime and had asked her not to. However, that would have been a much better alternative than this harrowing wait.

I stepped out on the pathway leading to the taxi stand. Finally, I reconciled myself for another fifteen-minute wait in the pre-paid queue for getting hold of a yellow-top taxi to take me to my Bandra residence. You've got to sit inside one to understand for yourself as to why people avoid them like the plague. They are not vehicles. They are a conglomeration of wheels, seats and engine, all put together to take the form of a rickety machine in motion.

Barely had I reached the middle of the road, when I froze. All eyes, including mine, turned from the airport exit point to the road which I had to cross to reach the taxi stand. I looked in that direction and my eyes popped out.

I could hear 'Oooh's' and 'Aaah's' emanating from the crowd behind me, but I could not turn back. My eyes were riveted on the main road ahead, and there she was....

Dressed in red, gleaming under the lights, demurely, she turned into the road that lead to the airport entrance and sashayed onto the black tarmac. She was heading towards me, but I just could not move. My legs were rooted and my mind was blank. She came to a halt a few metres from me. If she moved any further, she would have run over me. But heartless as she was, she did not.

Everyone crowded around to admire her. Even the cops came and stood around her, guarding her from groping miscreants. That did not work. A few gathered courage and touched her. She hardly seemed to mind. Neither did she scream, nor did she shout. She just stood there patiently, allowing everyone to admire her, touch her, and feel her!!!

I gathered some courage and walked up to her, I could make out the words 'Sachin Tendulkar' etched in small fonts. Now I knew!!!!

This was Tendulkar's Ferrari, a Ferrari Modena 360, gifted to him by Formula One Champ, Michael Schumacher in

England only a year ago. I tried to peek in through the dark window pane, no one was inside. Sachin Tendulkar was scheduled to return from London and the Ferrari was there to pick him up.

What a stroke of luck! Ferraris are not common in India and sighting them is an opportunity of a lifetime. This was the second time I had sighted a Ferrari. My entire exhaustion evaporated in a jiffy, my mood turned jubilant and when I turned towards the host of taxi drivers who had turned their back towards the airport exit to see the Ferrari, I even saw my name on a small placard. There it was!! I waved furiously to the driver, who came forward and apologised profusely. I returned home comfortably ... dreaming, all along the way, of the Ferrari. Would I own a Ferrari, ever? Only time would tell....

Three

It Gets Closer

I was in Hyderabad, in honour of our Hyderabad team having achieved record sales figures. It was quite a stressful day at work ... more so because I had to take the morning flight to Hyderabad, and I just hated morning flights.

I thought of retiring to the hotel room, when Nitin Chengappa, one of my colleagues at the head office came up to me and said, 'Ravi, we've a party tonight with the Hyderabad team.' Partying was the last thing that I was looking forward to. After two nights of partying and an early morning flight, my body was in the state of suspended animation. Despite my reluctance, I could not refuse. The whole team had been eagerly waiting for this evening. I

> ***Become a possibilitarian. No matter how dark things seem to be or actually are, raise your sights and see possibilities—always see them, for they're always there.***
>
> **NORMAN VINCENT PEALE**

decided to join them. This was my first visit to Hyderabad in my new job, and I was to motivate the team.

The bash was at Touch, a new chic pub in the heart of the city. A new pub, that too, owned by the reigning stars of the Telugu film industry, Nagarjuna and Amala, it had to have an aura of grandeur.

The party started at nine o' clock, well behind the scheduled time of 7.30 p.m. Jinesh (the national sales head), Nitin and I trooped in with the Hyderabad seniors at around 9.30 p.m.

The music rocked—predominantly Bollywood and Tollywood. If you have not heard of Tollywood yet, you must listen to the beats of Telugu songs to believe them. How on earth the heroes and heroines gyrate to these beats and keep their hips intact, remains a mystery.

The mood was groovy and liquor was flowing. I turned around and scanned the pub. Jinesh was busy doing 'bottoms up' with his sales team. He never touched alcohol. Quite amazing, it was, for a teetotaller to show so much of involvement when it came to getting people drunk.

Nitin was nowhere to be seen. I looked around to catch a glimpse of him, but could not. I assumed that he had stepped out for a phone call, or to the rest room. The music was getting louder and groovier every minute. The beats were getting all of us in a mood to dance. Time flew past, we hardly noticed.

'Ravi,' a whisper in my ears brought me back to reality. It was Nitin.

'Where were you? I was looking for you. You were the one who brought us here and you disappeared without even letting us know!'

'Come with me,' he continued, 'Now!' the stress on the word 'Now', worried me.

'Where? What's happened?'

Or, was this a diversionary tactic?

'Nothing has happened. Come, I'll tell you.' He sounded quite mysterious, but I decided to go along.

'What's it, Nitin?'

'I want you to meet someone.'

'Whom?'

'Sandy,' he said, as we entered the lift.

'Sandy! Who's Sandy?'

'He's an old friend of mine.'

'Do I know him?' No reply.

Why on earth would I need to meet an old friend of Nitin, I wondered, but out of courtesy, did not ask him. The lift stopped on the ground floor. It was half an hour past midnight.

Standing there in the lift lobby was a man in his early thirties. Hair cut extremely short and clothes which gave him away, he stretched his hand out towards me and said, 'Hi! I'm Sandy.' The looks were typically Andhra, but the accent was distinctly American.

So, this was the person Nitin wanted me to meet. 'Oh, Hi! Good to see you.' I hated the fact that I had to be nice to some unknown man in the middle of the night. I wanted to get back to Touch quickly, back to the music and my vodka. I looked at Nitin, wondering and at the same time, imploring him to tell me why he wanted me here at this hour.

'Come,' said Nitin and started walking towards the main gate. I had no choice but to follow. He stopped and turned back when he reached the gate. I had a 'clueless' look on my face when I had begun to follow him. Now, as he turned back and looked at me, my expression had turned to 'clueless and irritated'.

'Wanna go for a drive?' He said with a sly grin on his face. I could have killed him for that.

'Why on earth would I want to go for a drive at this hour, Nitin?'

Nitin sensed my frustration, so did Sandy. I turned towards Sandy, wondering what kind of joke it was. That was when I noticed Sandy lifting his hand pointing down the road. 'What do you say now?'

'Woooooow!' I immediately followed it up with a college Romeo kind whistle.

A few yards ahead, shining in the streetlights was a brand new, spotlessly clean Ferrari. Sandy had just invited me to ride a Ferrari ... was I dreaming! I pinched myself, I was awake after all. It would be my first chance to sit in a Ferrari.

Now, I knew why Nitin had dragged me away from the party. A ride in a Ferrari had been my desire for long. For nothing in the world I could have refused this offer.

I immediately walked towards the waiting car and got in. Sandy got into the driver's seat and said, 'Don't get nervous. I drive quite well.'

'I'm sure, you do ...' my sentence fading midway as he turned on the ignition and revved up the engine. The sound was awesome. The feel was great. The experience was pulsating. He pressed the accelerator and the rubber hit the road. As it cruised along the near empty road, the acceleration and the speed set my adrenaline racing. I was finally sitting in a Ferrari ... first time in my life.

We took a round and returned.

'Sandy, may I drive?' I could not resist asking him as we got out. He looked at me, then at Nitin, paused for a second and tossed me the key. 'Here. Drive carefully. It's not been insured yet.'

'Thanks, Sandy,' I muttered and got into the driver's seat. Nitin got in from the other side. Sandy could not, for it was a two-seater.

The engine purred as I turned on the ignition. The rest was pure ecstasy. Ten minutes of unadulterated driving pleasure and energy as I whizzed past the sleeping areas of Hyderabad. When I finally returned, I was in the least willing to return the keys, but I had to. The car was not mine, after all. It was someone else's Ferrari that I had driven. Nevertheless, I HAD driven a Ferrari!

Heaven on Earth is a choice you must make, not a place we must find.
WAYNE DYER

For days to come, every morning while driving my car, I remembered this drive. It was the high point of my visit to Hyderabad.

Four

The Changing Face of Time

30 May 2006

The Air Deccan flight from Mumbai to Thiruvananthapuram, DN 702 was scheduled to take off at 8.30 p.m. in the evening. However, till 10.30 p.m., there were no announcements of when the flight would take off, or if it would, at all.

I happened to book tickets for that flight. One does look for fare economies while going for a vacation, and I was no exception. Air Deccan was a low-cost airline in India and they offered excellent fares from Mumbai to Thiruvananthapuram on a night flight. I was heading to

It is not the strongest of the species that survive, nor the most intelligent, but the one most responsive to change.

CHARLES DARWIN

Maldives for my annual vacation with my family and the three of us were very excited. There was only one direct flight to Maldives from India. We would reach Thiruvananthapuram at 10.30 p.m., and after an overnight stay there, would take the morning flight to Male, the capital of Maldives.

The airport was crowded. Four Air Deccan flights were delayed. All the passengers converged around the small Air Deccan counter manned by two junior staff-members, who were on the verge of a nervous breakdown. The Air Deccan staff had absolutely no clue about the arrival and departure schedules.

The waiting lounge was full. An elderly couple sat down on the floor in the middle of the hall. They were too tired to stand. Other passengers, too, were getting restless. It was hot and humid and despite the air-conditioning, everyone was sweating profusely. The clock was approaching midnight at a feverish pace.

To be fair, Air Deccan could not be held responsible. Due to heavy monsoon showers in Kerala, flights could not take off on time, throwing the entire connecting schedule out of gear.

As the passengers started getting impatient, a security guard stepped in, '*Aap logon ko to pata hai, yeh roz ka haal hai. Phir ap isme ticket kyon lete hain* (You all know, this is a daily affair. Then why do you buy tickets on this airline?).'

The guard had intended to help by being sympathetic. Instead, he ended up instigating the crowd. A heated debate started on whether low-cost actually meant low service levels.

'Air Deccan, *Hai* ... *Hai*! Air Deccan, *Hai* ... *Hai*!!!' The chants started reverberating in the entire airport. The counter staff, sensing trouble, disappeared.

Suddenly, amidst the loud din and the crowd frenzy, I heard a tiny, delicate voice. 'Air Deccan, *Hai* ... *Hai*! Air Deccan, *Hai* ... *Hai*!!!!' It sounded like a sacred chant in a noisy pub, a sprinkle of cold water in the midst of a desert storm.

I turned to look behind me. Standing there holding her beautiful mother's right hand with her left, pumping her right hand in the air, as she joined the crowd in screaming, was a small, tiny little cherub. At most, she would have been six years old. Oblivious of the public gaze, she seemed to be enjoying herself, screaming herself hoarse.

Flashback to the year 2000: *The setting—Chennai airport. It was two in the afternoon. I was waiting outside the airport, waiting for the flight from Delhi to arrive. Thankfully, I was not made to wait in the sun for long. The flight was on time. Within fifteen minutes, a pretty young face made her way out of the airport holding a newborn, wrapped in a soft quilt. As she approached me, I stepped out from where I was standing, walked towards her and gave her a warm lingering hug. I bent down to look at the angel, blissfully asleep, gave her a peck on the cheek and then took her over from her mother and walked towards the parking lot where my Maruti 800 was parked. My wife and newborn, Anusha, had returned home from Delhi, where Dharini had gone for giving birth to our first child.*

Standing beside me at the Mumbai airport holding my daughter's hand firmly was my wife of twelve years, trying unsuccessfully to control my daughter as she continued with her chant 'Air Deccan, *Hai ... Hai*'. This was my daughter's first exposure to a public display of anger—though she was screaming more out of fun than anger.

Somehow, the flight took off at 1.30 a.m., and by the time we reached the hotel in Thiruvananthapuram, it was 4.00 a.m. We slept for a couple of hours and then caught the flight to Male, the next morning.

At the Thiruvananthapuram airport, as we were getting off the taxi to head inside, Anusha asked me, '*Appa*, which flight are we taking now?'

'Indian Airlines, Anusha. That's the only one which goes to Maldives.'

'Thank God! *Appa*, from now on, we'll not go by Air Deccan. I will only come by Jet or Kingfisher.' These were the leading airlines in the country. My wife looked at me and smiled.

'That's clever; for a six-year-old to know the good airlines from the bad ones.' She was thrilled.

I was not. For me the statement held a different meaning, something which made me uncomfortable, something way more serious than the battle between the low-cost and the luxury airlines, much more disturbing than the deterioration of Indian Airlines and Air India. Something, that evolved faster than the pace at which new airlines were entering the Indian air space.

I travelled by air for the first time when I was twenty-three years old. I was the first in my family to do so. My daughter travelled by air when she was twenty-three days old. And by six, she developed an idea about the airline company to select and the one to reject.

> *We always overestimate the change that will occur in the next two years and underestimate the change that will occur in the next ten. Don't let yourself be lulled into inaction.*
> *BILL GATES*

This took me back to the memory of my first flight from Bangalore to Delhi. Just as the plane was disappearing into the clouds, I had caught the fleeting glimpse of a Ferrari. A red Ferrari. And then, it disappeared. After fourteen years of toil and sweat, I was nowhere close to the Ferrari, and here was my daughter making demands of the airlines she wished to travel by.

Five

I Want My Ferrari

That night at Hyderabad, when I returned to my hotel room after the enchanting drive in the Ferrari, sleep had deserted me. I desperately wanted the Ferrari for myself. I had tasted blood. I had driven one.... Finally, when my eyes closed involuntarily at 4.00 a.m., I was still dreaming of the Ferrari.

The next day, by a streak of providence I happened to come across a copy of *The Monk Who Sold His Ferrari* by Robin Sharma at the airport. I had heard about the book, picked it up on an impulse, started reading it on the flight and continued reading

You are the person who has to decide.
Whether you'll do it or toss it aside
You are the person who makes up your mind.
Whether you'll lead or will linger behind.
Whether you'll try for the goal that's afar.
Or just be contented to stay where you are.

EDGAR A. GUEST

back at home. I skipped office that day to finish the book. It was about a hotshot lawyer, Julian Mantle, who, one fine day, sold off everything that he possessed—his island, private jet plane, mansion, even his new red Ferrari and headed to the Himalayas, where he met a sage, learnt lessons about life, and became a monk.

This made one fact of life appear more blatant to me than ever. In order to give up something you first need to possess it. Julian Mantle could give away his Ferrari because he owned one. He had achieved success in life and hence, could afford to transcend it.

It is true that success, i.e. material success is only one of the several strata of life that needs to be transcended for the fulfilment of the being. But to expand beyond success, to have the guts to discard it for greater realities of life, you must experience success first. The question is not of being a monk or a materialist; it is the question of self-realisation. There are different aspects of the Self, and all these aspects are necessary for self-realisation. Therefore, owning a Ferrari is important. Success, money and the associated lifestyle are important, as they help you to realise yourself, first and foremost, then of course, for your family, near and dear ones.

Before I move on, I would like to emphasise on something here. You must be wondering as to what a six-year-old girl's flying experience has to do with the Ferrari? What does the first flying experience of a twenty-three-year-old tell you?

It is not about flying. It is about changing lifestyles, cultures, expectations and hence, the changing pressures on all. It epitomises the way the world has changed over the last decade. When I passed out from IIM-Bangalore, not having travelled by air ever in life was not strange, but today it definitely will raise a few eyebrows.

Success, money and the associated lifestyles have never been more important. Social pressures, personal requirements, the need for maintaining a standard of living have never been so crucial. Even the pressures from family to maintain a certain status are at an all-time high. The needs and desires of children today are not similar to those when we were young. Today, demands have undergone a radical change. The difference is like chalk and cheese. Let me elaborate this with some instances.

In my school days, neither me, nor any of my friends were ever embarrassed about visiting their hometowns or villages during the summer vacations. In fact, summer vacations were meant to be family reunion sessions. I still remember, in my childhood days, I would trudge with my family all the way from Ludhiana, where we lived, to Trichy in Tamil Nadu, to meet my grandparents. It was partly because exotic vacations were a drain on your finances, and only a few had enough money to afford such luxuries.

But it is not so anymore. Try talking to your children on the first day after their vacations....

The conversations will only be about ... 'Dad, Prerna went to Switzerland for her vacations, Aashna went to America ... Kabir's parents took him to Disneyland.' What does this show? Peer pressure starts building up from within the school itself. God help you, if you had taken your child to Matheran, Mahabaleshwar or Nainital. You've had it. How will you live upto the expectations your children and family have of you if you are not successful?

Today, being successful is a pre-requisite for a happy family. Every child wants a successful parent; every spouse wants a successful spouse. If you are not in the league, or not directionally moving towards it, it becomes one of the reasons for conflicts to arise.

If you do not believe what I am saying, do this simple exercise. Ask your children, when they attain a sensible age if they would have preferred their parent to be the managing director of a company with a high pressure job which leaves him little time for the family; or if they preferred the parent to be a clerk with lots of time for their family, but hardly any money to take care of their worldly desires. If the answer is the latter, please do not read further—this book is not for you. I would be surprised if any one of you does that because my experience says that you will never get this answer.

The world has come a long way from what it was some two decades back. Needs have grown, so have expenses. People have graduated to more flashy and materialistic lifestyles. An iPod, a new Nokia mobile every year, an LCD TV, a flashy car to drive to work, a weekend movie, a designer outfit, a microwave for the kitchen, diamonds for every anniversary and birthday ... all cost money ... And wait, I have not even mentioned the kiddie stuff. Where will all this come from, if you are not successful?

In the book *It Happened in India,* Kishore Biyani, the head honcho at Pantaloons (now rechristened, Future Group) says, that if expenses grow, income is bound to grow. And, it will grow because you will work towards earning more, so that those expenses are sustained. The fact is that everyone spends more today than what he used to spend earlier or even what his parents had spent in real terms.

I do not know as to how many of you have realised the relevance, but in a nutshell, the Ferrari is more critical now than it ever was. Later in the book, I will spell out what exactly the Ferrari signifies, but very briefly, it signifies success, achievement, growth, wealth and well-being.

As you read through the next few chapters you will realise that this book is about success, about achieving success at your own terms, about achieving success and staying successful, about beginning to enjoy your success in life. This book is all about making that elusive Ferrari yours. How do you go about systematically making it your prized possession?

I presume that if you have reached this far, you are desirous of acquiring the Ferrari for yourself, one that you can proudly whizz away with, as the envious onlookers gather around you.

Now that I have your attention, it is time to move on to make the dream to acquire the Ferrari come true....

Ten Commandments

Six

Aspire High

> *You can fly*
> *With all the colours in the sky.*
>
> *You can soar.*
> *Don't think about your troubles anymore!*
>
> *You can glide,*
> *and forget about why*
> *you can't do this or that.*
>
> *You can dream!*
> *Though life may seem*
> *So hard sometimes,*
>
> *Get on with your life*
> *And just fly!*
>
> ANONYMOUS

It was the end of November 2006, I was planning out a birthday party for my daughter, which fell in December. I called in a few party planners, hoping to give her a birthday she would never forget.

I was quite surprised that birthday parties for children are no longer cheap these days. People make a living of them and, take my word, once you start talking to them, you realise that there is no end to the amount you can spend on activities which comprise a party. Theme parties, princess parties, club parties, chat parties ... there are endless number of things these party planners tempt you with. So much for a simple birthday celebration.

I fondly remembered the days when my mother arranged joint parties for my brother and me. Our birthdays were a month apart and mom would have a party around the end of January—this made up for both my brother's birthday in January and mine in February. Birthday parties, those days, involved inviting a few neighbourhood children, and cutting a homemade cake—which would be a conventional circle, triangle, or square in shape. We were served with Campa-Cola or some similar drink, if we were lucky. We would play games such as passing the parcel, musical chairs, etc. That would be it.

But things are different now. The first day the organiser met me, she handed me a long list of things she could possibly do for a party on my terrace. I selected some of them. Then she gave me a list of decors for the party. I selected some.

'Sir, would you like us to organise the food as well?'

I knew a decent south Indian caterer, so I said, 'I will take care of it.'

'And music?'

'What for?' I asked.

'The games that we'll play with the children need to be accompanied by music. And after that, won't they want to dance?'

I did not want to look like some Marwari businessman negotiating with her. Though not convinced I replied, 'Fine!'

'Sir, the music system and the DJ will cost you three thousand rupees for the two-hour party.'

I nodded. My daughter was all of six years. With an additional three thousand rupees I would have been able to buy a new 75W music system. However, I let that thought pass.

'You'll also need Power Cams.' This was the first time I had heard that word. What the hell were Power Cams?

As if reading my mind, she said, 'Power Cams are coloured lightings which give a chic look to the venue.'

'Okay.'

'For the Power Cams, you will need a 5KVA wiring and you need to provide us with a point for it.'

'God ... will it ever end?' I was cursing the day I got into this. Finally, after fifteen minutes, the discussion ended. The party planner got up and thrust a paper into my hands. When I glanced through it, I felt as if a thousand-volt current had passed through my body. I nearly fell off the chair. The paper had the charges for the event; 1,24,000 rupees for the birthday party and she had the audacity to mention that the cake would be charged extra.

After politely saying that I would get back to her, I quietly went into the bedroom and showed the paper to Dharini. Though rattled initially, she regained her composure and said, 'Why don't we do it at McDonalds or Pizza Corner, or in some small party hall?' I had aspired for a grand birthday party for my daughter and all of it was about to come to dust … well, just about to.

At last, we decided to ask Anusha. She should also have a say in selecting the venue of her birthday party. We had not told her about our plan to have it on the terrace. In fact, I was glad that I hadn't mentioned it.

'Anusha, what do you want for your birthday?'

'*Appa*, it's supposed to be a surprise. Don't ask me.' So far, so good.

'Okay. Where should we have your birthday party?' I expected a meek McDonalds, Pizza Corner, Inorbit Mall Game area, or at worst, Taj Lands End, as an answer. But what came was totally unexpected.

'*Appa*, last year we had it on the terrace. Can we have it somewhere else?'

'Like … where?'

'Goa!'

'What? Where did you say?' I helplessly hoped that I had heard it wrong.

'Goa!'

'Gooooaaa?' I was shocked. Where the hell did she get the idea of going to Goa for a birthday party!

'That's not possible.'

'Why?'

'I said NO!' I did not even want to argue on this.

'But why not, *Appa*?'

'Because *Appa* can't get leave to come to Goa and be with you on your birthday. If we have the party in Mumbai, he can be with you for most of the day.' This logic from Dharini worked. The issue was suspended for the time being.

But this got me thinking. It should get you readers thinking, too. The message is that if you wish to aim for the Ferrari, develop AUDACIOUS GOALS.

Once, I came across a small but very thoughtful quotation, embossed on a silver plaque. It read:

Some men see things around them and wonder why?
I dream of things that aren't, and say why not?

—George Bernard Shaw

To elaborate this further, let me tell you the story of a young starry-eyed girl, who once went to her father's office. Her father, the CEO of a reputed insurance company (India Trade and General Insurance Company Limited), left her alone in his room and went out for a meeting. Those days there were no computers and the little girl did not have anything to do. So, she climbed into her father's chair with great difficulty and sat down. The leather felt soft and luxurious. With her arms on the two arm-rests, feet propped up on the table—she was close to heaven.

She looked around the room, there was a nice lampshade placed in a corner, and a portrait of Jawahar Lal Nehru, on one of the walls. Thick green curtains covered the window which opened out to the busy M.G. Road, in the Fort area of Mumbai. She loved the setting, but she needed more excitement than this. And, it came in the form of one kick of the leg, and the chair went swivelling. 'Yippee!!!' she screamed happily. It was fun. Another lunge she gave, this time the left leg pushed the table and the chair swivelled in the opposite direction.

'What's going on?' Her CEO father had just returned and was standing at the door. He was clearly not amused at his room being turned into a playground.

'Nice chair, dad.'

'Hmmm ...'

'Dad, can I take it home?'

'No! Now come on, get off the chair.'

'Dad, why not?'

'I said, get off the chair. Come and sit on this sofa,' he said pointing to an exquisite leather sofa, set gallantly at one corner of the room.

'Okay. Dad, can I come to your office every day and sit on this chair. I just love it.'

'No, *beta*. That's not possible. Now, come on. I'll have to finish some work and we'll get back home. Mummy will be waiting.'

That day an aspiration was born—an aspiration to own an office, like the one her father had, an aspiration to head a large company, probably larger than that of her father's. The year was 1966. Over four decades later, everything that the little girl aspired for came true. When her father told her that she could not have the swivel chair that she wanted so much, she did not aspire just to get the chair all for herself. She aspired for much more. She dreamed of his office, his job and wanted to be the CEO of a large organisation, some day. She wanted to make a difference—she wanted to prove to the world that as a woman she was as competent as the men around her. Today, she has shown the world that an aspiration backed by self-will and belief can do wonders.

I chanced to meet this lady one day in her office, two years back. It was there that I saw G.B. Shaw's quotation, prominently displayed on her desk.

Naina Lal Kidwai, has earned her Ferrari ... the model she wanted, the colour she wanted and at the time when she wanted it. Today, she is the group general manager and the CEO of HSBC, in India. She followed her dreams and aspirations with such a passion that today she, as the CEO of one of the largest banks in India, sits in a large cabin, from where if she looks out, she would be staring at the same room where her father once sat, as the CEO of the insurance company, on the other side of the street—the room where her aspirations took birth. However, this is not her only achievement—she has been voted as one of the most powerful women in the corporate world by international magazines and newspapers like *Fortune*, *Time* and *Wall Street Journal*. Her moment of glory came in early 2007, when she was awarded the Padmashri, one of the highest civilian honours bestowed by the Government of India.

Naina aspired big. She was only sixteen when she dreamt of being a successful businesswoman, which in those days was considered to be a man's domain. She graduated from Delhi

University, where she had her first serious brush with leadership—earlier she had been elected the school captain at Loreto Convent, Shimla. She was voted the president of the Lady Shri Ram College Students' Union.

While doing her articles for Chartered Accountancy at Price Waterhouse Coopers, she realised that the only way to get ahead of men in this country was to be more qualified than them. So she set out on her journey. And, when she did set out, she aspired for the best. Despite resistance from her parents she went ahead and did her MBA from Harvard University. She was the first Indian woman to do so.

Notwithstanding lucrative offers to work overseas, she returned to India and joined ANZ Grindlays. In 1994, she joined Morgan Stanley and initiated the work on the merging of JM Financial and Morgan Stanley. In 2002, she joined HSBC and is today, the first lady CEO of any large foreign or private sector bank in India.

This is what aspiration can do for you. Set your aspirations high, chase them with wholehearted commitment and conviction—no one can hold you back. Naina's example proves this beyond doubt. She exemplifies the fact that if you want to own the Ferrari and be successful, aim high. Aim for the sky. Reach out for the stars and nothing lower. There will be a lot of people chasing and competing with you, if your aspirations are mediocre. But once you cut through the clutter and surge ahead, traffic is really very thin on the last mile. You will suddenly find yourself running all alone. Only a few people make the cut and if you want to be one of them, you will have to surge ahead with the power of your dreams.

Why is the story of the birthday party relevant here? In aspiring to have a birthday party in Goa at the age of six, Anusha was being restricted neither by the bias of people she knew, i.e. Dharini or me, nor was she limiting her thoughts to something mediocre. She wanted the best birthday party for herself and asked for it. Her request for a party in Goa might sound a bit naïve, but unless you aim big, you will never get anywhere. So, define your aspirations, state your goals, your objectives, all that you want to achieve and articulate them at least to yourselves. Once you ASPIRE and articulate it you are bound to reach the goal.

> *If you built castles in the air,*
> *your work need not be lost;*
> *there is where they should be.*
> *Now put foundations under them.*
> HENRY DAVID THOREAU

But what is the meaning of 'Aspire'?

ASPIRE to me is, **A Strategic Plan for Individuals which Revisits and Restates Expectations.**

A

Strategic

Plan for

Individuals which

Revisits and Restates

Expectations

All of us, at various points of time, at various levels, make strategic plans for businesses, departments, teams, etc. Once done with the initial planning the chain of action begins. Taking up necessary tasks to meet those goals come after that. If this can be done within an organisation, it can be done in life, too.

Your aspirations must be audacious and your efforts to achieve them must be commensurate with the audacity. Naina's story proves this point. She had the audacity and wanted to make the best out of it. She worked hard and concentrated all her efforts towards winning her laurel.

The harder you work, the more lucky you get.

THOMAS JEFFERSON

Today, Naina stands taller than most, rubbing shoulders with the polity and the regulators, businessmen and the media. She has carved a niche for herself in the banking world.

If you wish to get any closer to Naina's achievements, you will have to work hard at reaching your aspirations, blowing away all the obstacles that come your way. My recommendation is try out the CBA method, as Naina did, to acquire your Ferrari.

C – Constantly take stock of your aspiration

B – Balance between Success and Failure

A – Adopt an attitude to deal with situations.

Constantly Take Stock of Aspirations

Aspirations are dynamic. They keep changing every few years. Constantly taking stock of your aspirations means reinventing yourself. Ask yourself 'Where do I want to be? What do I want to achieve?' The answers to these questions must be constantly sought and revisited periodically to ensure that you are not pitching yourselves below your capabilities.

There are very few people who can conjure long-term visions and set themselves long-term goals. Most people cannot see more than three or four years ahead of them. A typical example is that of an executive in the branch of a small bank who aspires to be a branch manager. Once he becomes a branch manager, his aspirations change. He now aspires to become the head of a cluster of branches ... so on and so forth.

I can think of a similar paradigm in my early career. I joined ANZ Grindlays Bank in the year 1995 as a relationship manager, at a level which in those days was called Grade Three. All new management graduates joined at that level. The compensation structure in that level was a normal cash-based compensation with no perks attached to it.

However, things changed dramatically at the next level—referred to internally as a Grade Four position. As per the Human Resource rules, the bank offered a fully furnished accommodation, to anyone at Grade Four. Even the loan entitlement at that level was significantly higher. One could even get car loans at discounted rates of interest. My ultimate aspiration in life at that time was to get to Grade Four. I hoped that my life would change once I got there. I worked towards it and eventually did get there, but once I got there, everything changed—but not the way I had expected. Grade Four no longer sounded as alluring as it used to. Now, I wanted greater things in life. I wanted to ascend to Grade Five, Grade Six and Grade Seven. I wanted to progress. Had I become complacent, after reaching Grade Four, I would have remained there even now. Therefore, it is very important that you keep revisiting your aspirations and redefine them. Remember the definition of ASPIRE—A Strategic Plan for Individuals which Revisits and Restates Expectations—it sounds more sensible now, than ever.

Balance between Success and Failure

This is a very interesting point which Naina makes. Imagine you are setting sales targets for your teams. One of the teams busts its targets by the 25th of every month. This does not happen once or twice, but for months. Such a case has only one of two implications—either it is a brilliant sales team with tremendous drive, energy and passion that they are able to deliver a month's target in twenty-five days consistently, or that given their vintage, experience and calibre, the targets set for the team are just not good enough, so they are able to meet it easily. More often, the problem is the latter and not the former. Therefore, a word of caution for all those who have been successfully getting to hundred percent of their goals and aspirations ... maybe, you are not stretching yourself enough. You are setting far too low targets and are easily achieving them. If you can push your subordinates to stretch targets at the beginning of the year, you might as well do it for yourself while re-evaluating your goals.

Your quest for higher activations should not be tempered by your failures. To all those self-doubters, I would say that failure is not the end of the road. It is a learning opportunity. If you dissect every failure of yours, there are enough lessons to learn. You need not fear failure or public condemnation, after all. I can give you many instances of people who have failed and resurrected themselves from the ignominy of failure. They have gone along to become extremely successful in their pursuits of the Ferrari.

Let me tell you about a young cricketer. He was initially selected to the Indian cricket team that toured South Africa in 1991–1992. After a disastrous series, he was dropped from the team. He never made it back till he was picked up again for the series against England in 1996, wherein he made back to back centuries in his first two matches and even momentarily threatened Azharuddin's record of three consecutive centuries on debut. This was Saurav Ganguly who went on to become one of the most successful captains in the history of Indian cricket. Then, there was this young man, who was initially thrown out of the All India Radio auditions for his unusually heavy voice, thoroughly unfit for the job of a news-reader. Who would imagine that he was destined to become the most coveted voice in Indian film history—Amitabh Bachchan. You would not have heard these names if they had been deterred by failures.

However, the bottom line is, aim for the stars and reach them. That is what I call an aspiration fulfilled. You can stand on a stool and reach the ceiling quite effortlessly, but reaching the stars is not quite as easy. Owning a Ferrari never was.

Attitude to Deal with Every Situation

The path to the Ferrari will not be bereft of obstacles. There will be a number of cynics to condemn you. Eccentric, dreamer, impractical ... you will often find such words being thrown at you. A successful man is one who builds a strong foundation with the bricks that others throw at him.

When Bill Gates said, 'A PC on every table' in the early eighties when servers were of the size of half a room, people laughed. He was dismissed as a maverick. But look at where we stand today. A computer is an indispensable tool both in office and at home. Can you imagine a life without computers now? Therefore, reaching the pinnacle of your aspirations requires a special skill. An ability to deal with detractors and doubting Thomas's with confidence. The best way to deal with the detractors trying to dent your confidence is not to have them in your team at all. Build a team of people who will help you fulfil your dreams. Having a team full of aligned, strong-willed, and challenging individuals gives you the confidence to deal with almost any situation.

One of the big stories which held everyone's interest early in 2006, and which to my mind, marked the beginning of an era of India's economic dominance in the world, was the takeover of Arcelor Steel by Lakshmi Mittal. To date, I remember a television interview of L.N. Mittal, which was being telecast on CNBC TV18, soon after Arcelor had rejected the takeover bid of Mittal Steel, calling it hostile. It was in no way an easy interview, but Mittal kept his calm. The interviewer tried to push him hard to provoke a response. But Mittal would not say anything derogatory or controversial.

'Mr Mittal, what would you do if this deal does not go through,' finally the anchor asked him.

'Well ...' he paused 'for me, that option does not exist.' The confidence in himself, his team and his ability to fulfil his aspiration was very evident.

What makes this special was that, when he made this comment, the deal valued at $33.1bn, was far from being in his pocket. The entire European Union was against this deal. There were murmurs of racism which were gathering steam. It was a mammoth task Mittal was staring at. No one gave him a chance. Arcelor too, had found a suitor in Severstal (a steel company based in Russia) and the CEO of Arcelor and Severstal had gone on record and announced the proposed merger of Arcelor with Severstal.

Getting to the point of closure of the merger involved a bruising fight for Mittal. In January 2006, Mittal's offer of Euro 18.6bn offer for Arcelor was harshly and swiftly rebuked by Arcelor's management and a chorus of European politicians who criticised everything from his looks, to his language, to his mannerisms, to his Indian origin and the quality of his company's steel. Arcelor seniors refused to even meet with Mittal until a string of demands were met, and simultaneously orchestrated a Euro 13bn deal with Severstal of Russia. Despite all this, Mittal prevailed and managed to create a conglomerate which is the largest steel manufacturing unit in the world. He had the attitude and the confidence to deal with every situation and the faith in himself. Had he surrounded himself with a set of doubters, he would never have made this deal.

> *I dream my painting and then paint my dream.*
>
> VINCENT VAN GOGH

The Ferrari is a dream … a desire … a passion. You need extraordinary skills to acquire it. It is not for the ordinary lot. To get there you need to set your goals high and go after them with a singleminded and a fearless dedication: the way in which Naina pursued her aspirations.

COMMANDMENT ONE

To acquire the Ferrari you need to ASPIRE.
And when you aspire, do not compromise
for anything but the best.

Seven

Stay Positive

It was a Saturday afternoon, Dharini and I decided to go out for a movie. With Anusha in tow, we settled on *Ta Ra Rum Pum*, the latest Hindi blockbuster, from the Yashraj Films banner. With Anusha around, we normally avoid the late night shows, and hence, matinee show it was. The movie was very emotional and for the first time I saw my little one cry in a theatre. She was extremely touched by all that the children in the movie went through and did for the sake of their parents.

One ship drives east and another drives west
With the selfsame winds that blow
'Tis the set of sails and not the gales
Which tells us the way to go.
ELLA WHEELER WILCOX

The movie got over at six in the evening, and after stepping out of IMAX Multiplex at Wadala, we walked into the Crossword Bookstore within the same complex. As we were going through the books someone called out my name.

'Hey, Ravi! What a pleasant surprise!'

I turned around, and found a middle-aged man, standing right next to me, grinning from ear to ear. Seeing a blank look on my face he hastened to add, 'I'm Paresh! Don't you recognise me?'

'Oh yes, of course. How could I forget you, Paresh?'

Paresh, my batch-mate at IIM-Bangalore, was extremely studious who always ranked among the toppers. If my memory serves me right, he ranked third in the batch of 180 students. Very intelligent. He had come there with his daughter, who was a little older than Anusha.

We started talking. Except for some extra pounds around his midrif, he looked just the same. He resided somewhere in Bandra, very close to my home so I offered to drive them back, which he accepted. On the way back, he invited me to his house for a quick drink before heading back home. I turned to look at Dharini and Anusha to check if it was fine with them. Anusha was insistent on playing with Paresh's daughter, so I dropped Dharini, Anusha and Paresh's daughter at our house and went back with him for a drink.

I could make out from his body language that he had been through a fair bit of stress in life. He was living alone with his daughter, which was rather unexpected. Though he did not say much initially, he opened up after a few drinks. Apparently, his wife had left him and gone back to her parents about two years back. It was in no way a happy marriage to start with, and then to add woe to his worries he lost his job.

Paresh was working in the retail business of BNP Paribas. One day at work, he was called along with a few of his colleagues into the conference room. Initially, it appeared to be a normal meeting. But once inside the conference room, they were all given an envelope with a cheque of three months' salary as notice pay and their services were terminated. BNP was retreating from the retail business that they had got into only a few years back and they retrenched almost all their staff in the retail business. Paresh was one of the unfortunate lot. He was a victim of circumstances, of the faulty and hasty strategy of an organisation.

This proved to be the proverbial last straw which broke the camel's back. When he returned home and announced that he had lost his job, his wife went hysterical. Paresh was not wrong in seeking support on this traumatic day. But his wife was only adding to his misery. His thoughts were disrupted when he felt someone tugging at his kurta. It was his daughter Avantika. She stood next to him with a worried look on her face. He picked her up and nestled her on his lap.

'What happened, daddy?'

'Nothing, *beta*.'

'Why is mummy upset?'

'Nothing Avani, daddy's office has closed down. So, daddy has no job now. He'll not have to go to office anymore. So Mummy's worried.'

'Yeeeeeaaa! What fun!' Paresh glared at her but Avantika did not stop. She was running around with joy screaming 'Yeeeeaaaooow!!'

'Avantika, Stop it!' screamed Paresh.

'Dad, so you will not go to office?'

He nodded.

'Yippeee! You will be with me throughout the day.' Little did Avantika realise that this innocuous statement of hers would change her father's life forever. Her words struck Paresh like lightning. He was worried about the direction his life was taking and his daughter had already given him a reason to fight back. She had found a positive streak in what he thought was the end of the world. She found a reason to be happy amidst the gloom. The reason for her joy was that Paresh would now be with her throughout the day ... something she had been yearning for long.

This simple incident changed Paresh's entire perspective of looking at life. He understood that life always has a positive streak in it. It is just a matter of finding it out. It may seem to be a search among the ruins at the beginning, but once it is found it lasts forever. It becomes a habit, an imbibed culture. That was what happened to Paresh. After the incident, he started looking at life positively, and resolved to be happy, always.

Often, when you set out to acquire the Ferrari, you will encounter nerve-wrecking obstacles. It is important, that you remain optimistic even on the face of such crisis.

There is a legend of a saint who met three workers building a temple at the foothills of Himalayas. The terrain was rough and the weather was harsh. The workers were sweaty and tired but laboured away. It was not an easy task. The saint was thirsty, so he stopped for some water. While he was filling water in his sack, the first worker came along.

Overcome by curiosity, the saint asked him, 'What are you doing, my friend?'

'I am laying the bricks.' He drank water from the tap and went away.

The saint then walked up to the second worker and asked him the same question.

He answered, 'I am trying to earn money to meet my ends.'

The saint went to the third worker to ask him as well.

'I am building the largest temple anyone has ever seen,' he replied.

All the three workers were working on the same temple, but with different perspectives. The third worker was probably the happiest and at total peace with himself. The difference between him and the other two was that he had a long-term vision, a wider perspective in envisaging the end result of his creation; therefore, he enjoyed his work. The others saw it as something which had to be done and resigned themselves to their fate. The third worker had positive thought and high aspiration, which the other two lacked.

Let me tell you about P. S. Jayakumar, the head of sales and distribution for Citibank in India. He joined the bank in 1986 and had been with the organisation for over fifteen years. He was responsible for four business-lines of Citibank (personal loans, mortgages, auto loans and liability sales) and was one of the senior most employees of the bank. A very influential person indeed, within the Citibank circle.

> ***A rock pile ceases to be a rock pile the moment a single man contemplates it, bearing within him the image of a cathedral.***
>
> **ANTOINE DE SAINT**

A man of superior capabilities, Jayakumar was way ahead of his colleagues. At meetings, he would come up with revolutionary ideas beyond anyone's bandwidth. In the year 2001, Jayakumar was talked about as the next head of retail bank for Citibank in India. An invincible contender for the post, he was, surely. But luck would not have it. Jayakumar's long-term adversary, based in London, moved in as the head of retail bank, dashing all his hopes to the ground. Jayakumar was left stranded. Adding insult to injury was the fact that he had to report to the new head.

In the year 2001, Citigroup carried out a worldwide acquisition of a company called The Associates. This company operated in the sub-prime lending space, which was at the opposite end of the spectrum as far as Citigroup was concerned. Citibank targeted the elite, and The Associates targeted the lower-end of the income pyramid. Hence, this acquisition made Citigroup's business appear complete. They now had products targeted at every individual across the economic spectrum.

In India, The Associates was a small company operating in around ten cities with about fifteen branch offices. It was a very well-managed company, and when Citibank took it over, it had over five hundred employees.

About the same time, after taking over The Associates, Citibank wanted its own leadership team to run the company, in line with what any acquiring company does. This was necessary for seamless and cultural integration of the acquired company with the acquirer.

Now the mantle fell on Jayakumar. He was asked to give up his current post as the head of sales and distribution to take over as managing director of The Associates. He, whose job involved managing sales of auto loans, mortgages, personal loans and bank branch sales, was, for obvious reasons unhappy. From his current role, coming down to the position of a managing director of a small company like The Associates, was seen to be a step back as far as his career was concerned. He was disheartened … who would not be? Everyone perceived this to be a vindictive act on the part of the new retail bank head. Jayakumar's boss left him with no choice, he had one of the two option—either do as his boss said or leave the organisation.

Imagine being faced with a similar situation. Everything is going on just fine. People like you, respect you, think you to be great and then … struuuuutttt … sttruuuuurr … you stutter and stop. Many would probably start whining. The obvious responses would have been: 'Oh my gosh!!! … How could he do this? … What does he think of himself? … Am I not good enough? … I'll Quit!' The last one is the mother of all reactions. The earlier reactions create a frame of mind that culminates in the final exclamation.

In such a situation your initial emotion is anger, which turns to wallowing in self-pity, generating loads of negative energy and heated comments like, 'This organisation sucks'... and finally comes desperation. The result is a quick stride through the exit door and an equally fast entry to the first organisation that offers a job. Is this the right approach? Well, the answer is YES, if you are an escapist, who runs away from challenges. This is the easiest getaway, from detractors, adversaries, and the perceived failure. But often, this proves to be the blunder of a lifetime. Because under duress, the decision-making ability tends to get clouded by the desperation to run away.

But, if you want the Ferrari for real, you need to have the drive and the determination to fight and ward off all such challenges. There are two ways in which you can do that. Either you can stay and work your way out so that you get your due and your rightful place back, or, you try and make the best of whatever comes your way so that people are forced to sit up and take notice of you.

> ***The moment of enlightenment is when a person's dreams of possibilities become images of probabilities.***
>
> **Vic Braden**

Coming back to Jayakumar's case, he was a tough nut to crack. He decided to follow the second route. Make no mistake;

he was extremely annoyed with the treatment meted out to him by the organisation he had served for fifteen years. When his new 'boss' told him that he had to move, it came as a big, big surprise to him. It was very clear that some of his colleagues, unhappy with his growing influence conspired against him to move him out to a non-descript position. The emotional turmoil that Jayakumar went through was no different from what anyone else would have gone through. However, the final take was different.

Unfortunately, his exodus to The Associates was a double whammy. He was unceremoniously shunted out of Citibank to The Associates and the people at The Associates viewed him as an outsider ... a Citibanker in their midst, he was not accepted within The Associates. It was quite natural for the employees of an acquired company to feel threatened by an employee of the acquirer, especially if he has come in to manage the integration process. This built up the frustration level in Jayakumar. But for him there was no option but to stay on and fight.

The first few days at The Associates were like a nightmare, with a herd of hostile and unsupportive colleagues. The head office of The Associates was in Delhi, whereas Jayakumar's family was based in Mumbai. This made things more difficult for him. But he did not give up. He did not allow himself to be cowed down by negative feelings. He always felt that he could make it big. And that reflected in his demeanour, it was evident in his interactions with people. He started thinking as to how fruitful he could turn this opportunity into.

Soon, he discovered the fissure, the slack in the system of The Associates. He started penetrating deeper into it. The business model of the organisation was different from Citibank, so was the customer segment. Citibank was a bank for the elite, whereas The Associates operated for the low-income groups. A typical customer would not even walk into a Citibank branch, leave alone banking with them. Jayakumar realised, in a country of 1,200 million people, the only long-term way to build a franchise and sustained profitability was to serve the lower-middle class and The Associates was operating in that segment. The potential of this business was limitless, which Jayakumar's shrewd mind could easily envisage. He formed his own management team—a team of believers, of likeminded people. Once he got his marshals together, he went about re-engineering the company, changing processes, controlling the expenses and went on an unprecedented expansion spree. The company, which was operating with fifteen branch offices when he took over its control, in the next three years, opened over four hundred branches. Revenues started rising. The company started its journey towards being a profitable venture.

Jayakumar believed that he could do it and he went all out to achieve the goal.

In the meantime, all other businesses which Jayakumar was managing in Citibank, prior to migrating to The Associates, went downward on the scale. The loan margins were under pressure and the product profitability was under threat. However, The Associates' business which Jaya took over, later rechristened as CitiFinancial, continued to rake in money. Today the business where Jayakumar was shunted out to is the largest and the most coveted business for Citigroup in its entire retail franchise. That is not all. CitiFinancial is one of the largest consumer finance companies in this country.

And, Jaya is back as Citibank's head of retail bank in India after a short stint as the regional head of consumer finance for the group in the Asia-Pacific region. He is now viewed as the father of consumer finance in India and is one of the most sought after names in retail finance.

For a moment, sit back and imagine what would have happened if Jayakumar had decided to throw in the towel and run away from the crisis? Had he allowed the negative thoughts to cloud his mind and quit Citibank, none other than he would have lost out on the bargain. Would Citigroup have lost out on anything? Of course, not. Often, people make the mistake of assuming that they are indispensable for their organisations.

The truth is that no individual is greater than the organisation itself. Had he left Citigroup and joined some other organisation, Citibank would have appointed someone else in Jayakumar's post and everything would have progressed at a normal pace.

Would Jayakumar's adversary who pushed him into The Associates have been the loser? Not at all!! He would have got someone as his replacement and moved on. All the businesses would have got back on track in a few months. And, Jayakumar would have been a forgotten man.

All this could have happened had he allowed negative thoughts to cloud his judgement. But he did not do that. It is because he saw the silver lining even behind the darkest cloud; he is an immortal name in the annals of consumer finance in India.

He is now closer to the Ferrari than he ever was.

Everything will not go in your way ... it is not supposed to—life is like that. So, do not even bother to crib if things take wrong turns. Instead, just set it right and move on in life. A mistake that parents often make is to tell their children that everything in life is fair. This raises expectations. It is imperative to advise them to have an optimistic outlook, if they want to succeed in this competitive world. If in life, a tricky situation pushes you too hard against the wall, always look for a crack to break through, as Jayakumar did.

Remember, a single streak of optimism can charge an entire team. Wonder why people want to be surrounded by those who laugh away their woes rather than the crybabies? Simply because tears are contagious, and, I am sure, no one likes to crib and whine ... neither do you.

In conclusion, it is up to you whether you will whine and lose out on everything, or laugh and whizz away with your Ferrari.

COMMANDMENT TWO

Be optimistic; chase the negative thoughts away.

A positive frame of mind will surely get you closer to your Ferrari.

Eight

Be a Winner, Not a Wimp

Once I was invited for a formal dinner party at Taj Lands End, a posh five star hotel in the suburbs of Mumbai. It was hosted by the CEO of the bank I work for, attended by almost all the employees along with their spouses.

I told Dharini about the dinner. Her first reaction was, 'What should I wear?' A million dollar question to which, I never had a suitable answer. Women would invariably wear what they felt like, but would continue poking their spouses till they get the answers that they want.

> *The heights of great men reached and kept,*
> *Were not obtained by sudden flight,*
> *But they, while their companions slept*
> *Were toiling upward in the night.*
>
> Henry Wadsworth Longfellow

'Ravi, it's your office party. I have to look good.' I knew

where the the conversation was headed. She wanted a new outfit for the party. I grimaced at the thought of another expense, but did not want to get into an argument. They are, all married men would agree, best avoided in such situations. My silence was assumed as consent and a new outfit did arrive. I was in half a mind to ask the CEO to pay for it. On that Saturday evening, we went to the party, hand-in-hand, very much like a 'made for each other' couple. The party was just about warming up. People were still arriving. This was an annual reunion of sorts where everyone came with their families.

As we walked in, we met Suneel. A young man in his mid-thirties, he had been with the bank for over seven years. His wife was with him. I introduced Dharini to them and casually asked, 'All's well?'

'*Nahin yaar. Bahut phati hui hai* (No. All is not well).'

'Why, what happened?'

'*Arre, kuch nahin yaar* (Nothing much). Too much of work. I don't get to spend time with my family,' he looked at his wife and with his left arm around her waist, hugged her fondly. It looked like honeymoon had not yet ended.

'He doesn't come home before nine,' she complained. 'Even at home he is constantly on his Blackberry.' I tried to smile. The discussion then drifted to the Blackberry.

The last seven years Suneel had been with the bank, he had spent at the same grade. No move, no promotion. Partly, because he did not want to move and mostly, because no one wanted him in his or her team.

'Why?' Picking up from where we left.

'Work just doesn't seem to get over. These conference calls and meetings, they drain you out. And, you know Sangeeta. She's a perfectionist. Never happy with anything—pain in the neck she is. Makes us re-do everything.' Sangeeta was his boss. I just nodded at his remarks.

'If I had a business of my own, and worked so hard, I would have become a millionaire by now.'

'Sure. I am sure you would. You slog all day long. Had you slogged for yourself and not the organisation, you would have made enough money by now,' I said. All through, wondering what the consequences would have been like if had he been working for himself—maybe bankrupt by now.

I moved on. At a large party like this, it was important to move around so that you get noticed by all. I met another colleague of mine, who had joined the organisation recently. He used to work in a local bank where he had been working for the last twelve years before joining this bank.

'Hello ... Rohit.' I stopped as he came in front. 'How are you? Hope all's well?' I asked again.

'Ya ... but ...' he paused.

'But what?' The apprehension in his tone made me curious.

'It's extremely hectic here. No time for anything else.'

'But, what else do you want to do?'

'Look Ravi, I don't have enough time for my family. When I get back home, my son is already asleep. I hardly get to spend quality time with him. Life sucks, man.'

Rohit had joined the organisation only two weeks ago and he was already complaining. He was just about learning the tricks of the trade and had not yet got into his groove. What would happen if he got into his full-fledged workload and the related stress? I must confess, I was a bit taken aback by his response. Rohit had come alone and we were talking of businesses. Dharini was getting bored and that meant trouble. Sensing it, I moved on.

Ahead of me, as my eyes were panning the room, I saw a man—tall, middle-aged and slightly steely looking with a stylish golf cap on his head, and an exquisite red and blue silky scarf tied trendily around his collar. He was walking around the hall with the latest Nokia communicator in his hand, greeting all the seniors of the bank. I saw him and walked up to him. I tapped him on the shoulder.

'Have we met before?' I asked as he turned around.

'*Naah* ... I don't think so ... have we?'

'You look like someone I know,' I shook my head.

'Had you been a few kilograms lighter I would have recognised you. Now I can't,' he started laughing, so did I.

We had worked together when I was in Delhi and back there, we would meet almost every day. Our laughter caught notice of several others and soon, we were surrounded by a group of another six.

'How are you, Raj?' I asked him as the laughter subsided. I was seeing him after six months.

This gentleman, Raj Khosla was a leading service provider for the bank I worked in Delhi. He had a small firm that ran various accounting errands for all and sundry, before he started off with the bank in 1990. He would manage some small-time audits and other minor jobs for the bank. He had a small dingy office in Khan Market in Delhi. With time, he began to source a few two-wheeler loans and other cash loans for the bank. In the last decade, he had turned that dingy office manned by a few employees into a mammoth organisation which now boasts of over four thousand employees, providing Citibank with almost all the services, that he is permitted by the banking regulations. Had the bank regulators been benevolent to foreign banks in India, he would have done a lot more. The bank's reliance on him had reached to such a level that over ninety percent of the business in North India was originated by him.

The business he brought for the bank was probably higher than most of the banks in the private sector. This was a commendable achievement, indeed.

Someone from the crowd, tapped his shoulder and said, '*Aur* Khosla, what's happening?'

'*Bas lagey hue hain*. Business is rocking.'

I had met three men at the dinner party—Suneel, Rohit and Raj Khosla. And, see the difference! Two of them turned around and gave me reasons why 'life sucks' and here was a man who, for the same question oozed out so much vivacity, that there was nothing more to ask for. However, it was not the statement alone, but the attitude, the approach, the air of confidence, and the positive move, that gave a much better feeling.

Let me tell you more about Khosla. Raj Khosla, to put it loosely, is a DSA (Direct Sales Agent) for the bank for personal loans, credit cards, home loans and almost anything and everything under the sun—and he single-handedly calls the shots. He also does some outsourced work for the bank. It is a very stressful job. Apart from his own people, he has to deal with the business heads from the bank and their representatives who work with him, and of course, his own four thousand employees. He runs his office under the brand name of Shelters.

His day at work begins at 11.00 a.m. Once he enters his office he normally stays there unless something shakes him out. He does not even step out to the bank to meet the business heads. 'That's not my job,' he says modestly.

Throughout the day he interacts with the sales managers from the bank who help him manage his channels and his employees helping him extract productive work from all of them.

Every evening, without fail, when other offices close and bankers head home, he takes all his unit managers up on the terrace of his imposing office. There, they discuss short-term and long-term tactics and ways to combat competition, to recruit people from outside, to improve upon the management and derive the maximum from the bank know-how. This goes on till ... well, there is no limit. At times, he shares a drink with them on the terrace. What he does through this is figuring out for himself, who are the ones in his team ready for the next level opportunity and those who need to be got rid of.

These terrace discussions and his many other interactions has thrown up many a star. He has picked up people from nowhere, people who have been doing nondescript jobs, and backed them with larger roles. You will hardly hear of anything close to this in a small (if you can call it small) organisation. This would not have been possible had he not made the time and effort in working with his team.

Once he is done with the discussion on the terrace, he heads either to the Golf Club, or back to his office to meet with various people from the bank who manage his relationship—well, without him the bank would do no business, so they have to ensure that they assist him in managing it well. By the time he returns home it is about eleven at night. This happens day after day, month after month, year after year. … And, all seven days a week.

He claims that he is not a managing director but a chief motivational officer–a CMO. The only job he does the entire day, as he says modestly, is to ensure that none of his four thousand people leave. If anyone does, he takes it as a challenge and works to hold back the employee. And to give him credit, the attrition levels in his organisation, which many call a 'mom and pop show' is much lower than any large organisation with four thousand employees. Such is the commitment and dedication of this man. His hard work, and 'walk the talk' with his team has encouraged ordinary people in his team to dream big. Raj has, within Shelters, built a culture which he personally oversees, which motivates his four thousand employees to rise and achieve those dreams. People from ordinary backgrounds deliver extraordinary results with him, and he works throughout the day with them, making this happen. This takes its toll, leaving him with no free time for himself.

Till date, I have never heard him complain about trying to strike a balance between work and his family. I have never heard him say 'life sucks'. He has never complained of not being able to go back to his son every night. Though he too, has family responsibilities and aging parents to take care off, he has never let that affect his work. Does this mean that he has no love for his family? Of course, not. He is as much concerned about family, as he is about work. It is just that he is equally passionate about both.

Now, let me pose a different question to you. Assume for a minute that you have the Ferrari. You struggled in life, made it big and finally have acquired that dream machine. That is the only car you have. Would you stop driving the Ferrari on weekends because you need to give it some 'work-life' balance? The answer would be an absolute NO. If the answer is 'no' for the Ferrari, why should you be so bothered about 'work-life' balance for yourself?

I spoke of Khosla to prove one crucial point—if he can work fourteen to sixteen hours a day in his fifties, I am sure, the youngsters of today can do it as well. I have a piece of advice for those who have just made their career beginnings. If you want the Ferrari, and want it early in your career, you will have to take one of the three routes ... hard work, hard work and more hard work.

The other day, I had gone to IIM-Bangalore for a pre-placement talk—a presentation which every company makes to its prospective employees, telling them what it has to offer. I had gone to do a selling job—to sell my bank to the smart young MBAs. I could not curb my natural instinct and was showing off a bit during my talk. Digressing from the laid out presentation, I decided to demonstrate my audience-engaging skills. I looked at a young girl sitting quietly in the first row, I asked her, 'What would you look for in a company before you decide to join it?'

I caught her a bit off-guard and she was too baffled to answer. However, someone from the back did ... '"Work-life" balance!' My heart sank. I ignored the answer and asked for more parameters that would influence their choice of career ... 'Five-day-week!' Oh, my gosh! What is wrong with them? I decided to quickly shelve my digressive path and return to the original canned presentation.

It has become an 'in-thing' to talk of 'work-life' balance. In the good old days, when I studied at the same campus, answers to similar sounding questions would have been—exposure, learning, brand value etc. None of these featured in the top of mind response that I got. This 'work-life' balance has become the most discussed issue in the campuses as well.

But, I call it nothing more than just an idle topic for café gossip. Else, all the students would have run to join PSU (Public Sector Units). But that seldom happens. And, in that particular year not a single student joined a PSU.

Your Ferrari will not come with a 'work-life' balance. I once read an interesting interview, I think, it was with Rahul Bajaj, who said: '*"Work-life" balance is for wimps. Successful people go out and do what it takes to get there. If they have to work twenty-six hours out of twenty-four, they will.*'

Let me introduce a concept here—the **LFL** (**i.e. Leaders, Followers and Laggards**) rule of employee distribution. Every employee in an organisation falls in one of these three categories:

Leaders

Leaders are the scarcest of the lot. Barely five to seven percent of the people fall into this category. The organisation depends on this set of people to lay out the vision and direction. These people barely care about 'work-life' balance. They do what they have to do, irrespective of the organisational rules. If they have to give up their family temporarily to meet the demands of work, they will. If they have to slog seventy-five hours a week, they will.

A survey on the 'work-life' balance of CEOs by Grant Thornton International Business Report (IBR), published in *The Economic Times* states that Indian CEOs work the longest hours amongst all the CEOs in the world. Does it not automatically set expectations that they will have of their colleagues?

No organisation can motivate its leaders with 'work-life' balance initiatives. They do not need any.

Followers

This is the category where the maximum number of people fit in. They are the people who are satisfied with following instructions from the leader. Leaders lead and the followers follow them. The followers are happy with five-day week, limited working hours, family day initiatives, etc. No organisation can afford to ignore this lot because all organisations run on this category. The leaders are the thinkers and the followers are the doers. They implement what the leader asks them to. A few of these also graduate to a leadership status as they go ahead in life. And, it is quite surprising that the so-called leaders and senior managers of various organisations would fit in this category.

Laggards

Forgive me for this, they are the 'useless junks' in any organisation. Absolutely worthless but they still manage to tag with the company because no one has figured out yet that they are absolutely useless. About ten to thirteen percent of the employees in every organisation would be in this category. Laggards have a great personal life. Their contribution to work is almost negligible. Any 'work-life' balance initiative targeted at them will be a disaster, because they already enjoy enough of it. How early can you send a person home, who watches his clock everyday and leaves at six o'clock sharp?

Before proceeding any further, I would like to assure you readers that not for a minute am I propagating that organisations should not advocate 'work-life' balance. By all means they should. However, the laggards do not need any, and the leaders will not want any, but yes, the followers will. And, therefore, 'work-life' balance initiatives are important from an organisations' perspective, since they cater to the instincts of the followers, who bring up a significant portion of the employee population.

The Ferrari is not meant for everyone. It is neither for the average worker, nor for the followers, definitely not for the laggards. It is only for the leaders. And, as a matter of fact, it is for the best among the leaders. If you are one of those who moan and groan about 'work-life' balance, long hours at work, and not being able to see your family before ten at night, then sit snug on your sofa and relax. The Ferrari is not for you. Do not even try to get there, because I assure you, you will not!

COMMANDMENT THREE

Do not whine and whimper about 'work-life' balance. Be the winner, not the wimp, and the Ferrari will be yours.

Nine

Be Honest to Yourself

As a child, I heard the story of a monkey and a crocodile. They lived on opposite banks of a river and were great friends. Every day the monkey would pluck sweet fruits from trees and throw them into the river and the crocodile would gather and take them home to his wife. At night, the crocodile and his wife would savour those fruits. One day his wife asked the crocodile, how he got all the fruits. And the crocodile told his wife about his friend, the monkey.

> *Sow a thought, and you reap an act;*
> *Sow an act, and you reap a habit;*
> *Sow a habit, and you reap a character;*
> *Sow a character, and you reap a destiny.*
>
> ANONYMOUS

'If the fruits that the monkey gives you are so sweet, imagine how sweet the heart of the monkey would be. Can you get it for me?' She was beginning to salivate. The crocodile was aghast at the suggestion and rebuked her for harbouring such a thought. A few days later when the crocodile returned home, his wife was lying on the bed, shivering and sick.

She said, 'The doctor was here. He told me that I'll recover only if I eat the heart of a monkey, else I'll die.'

The crocodile was very worried and did not know what to do. He loved his wife and now she was forcing him to choose between his friend and her life.

That evening he invited the monkey for dinner. The poor monkey did not suspect anything and hopped on to the crocodile's back as he waded across to the other bank. Midway through the journey, under pangs of guilt, the crocodile told the monkey the real story. In any case, he was in the middle of the river and the monkey could not swim.

'Oh, is that all, my friend. I'd be glad but I've left my heart back on the tree itself. Had I known, I'd have carried it.'

'Oh God! What should we do now?'

'Let's go back. I'll quickly bring my heart down.'

So, the crocodile and the monkey made their way back to the shore. When they were near the shore, the monkey leaped to the safe confines of the tree, 'Foolish crocodile,' he said, 'I gave you all the fruits as a good friend, and now you want to kill me because your wife wants my heart. I'm not going back with you.'

When the crocodile's wife saw him returning without the monkey, she left him. The poor crocodile lost both his best friend and his wife. All because, he was not honest to himself.

This apparently simple story gives us a very important message. Dishonesty will always come back to haunt you. We have all lied at some point or the other in our personal and professional lives.

Calling in sick at work, lying about the reasons for your kids missing school, false excuses for being late for a meeting, buying a movie ticket in black ... the list is endless. These examples may apparently seem harmless, but they demonstrate an inherent tendency to lie and are, in a way, indications of bigger improprieties.

If we do something which is right, we will always benefit from it. But, dishonesty or any other misdeed for that matter will continue to haunt us throughout our lives.

At this juncture, step back and peek into the lives of winners, i.e. in the lives of people who are successful, who have made a mark for themselves in this world. You will find one common streak in all of them—all of them have the ability to stand up and face the consequences of their action. They will never do anything behind the back. They will not pussyfoot on tough decisions. Most importantly, they will follow deep-rooted moral values. They will never compromise on their values for a few rupees more.

Just, a few days back I read a book, *There is No Such Thing as "Business" Ethics* by John C. Maxwell. Maxwell rightly argues that when it comes to ethics there can be no double standards. You cannot set different standards for your personal and professional lives. What is ethical in one's personal life is ethical in business, too. And, as far as ethics is concerned, two things are important—the necessity of an ethical standard and the will to follow it. He says that Integrity is all about meeting the challenge of doing the right thing even if it costs more than what we want to pay.

> ***What lies behind us and what lies ahead of us are tiny matters compared to what lives within us ... a culture, a practice, a religion, something which all winners imbibe.***
>
> **RALPH WALDO EMERSON**

INTEGRITY AND ETHICS is all about a way of life ... which I am afraid is now becoming extinct.

How many times have you walked out of a store because you felt that the shop owner was trying to cheat you? If you ever drove into a petrol station and got an uncomfortable feeling that the oil is adulterated, will you ever go back to the same filling station again? Then, what makes you think that people, if they get a similar impression about you, would want to come back and deal with you?

I want to share an incident happened the other day. My wife and I walked into an electronics store in Bandra, an upmarket suburb of Mumbai. I wanted to buy an LCD television set and was looking for a large one. The salesperson showed me a large 46" television set and took me through all the features of the exotic looking Sony Television. I was nearly sold on it set till I realised that the one he was showing me was a Plasma television, despite telling him that I wanted an LCD television. When I reiterated to him that what I wanted was not a Plasma television, he went on to inform me that he did not have a 46" LCD television set in stock. It could well have been that he genuinely was trying to sell me a Plasma and had no mal-intent. I would have probably given him the benefit of doubt too, had he not told me that he did not have LCDs in stock. But now it seemed as if he was trying to sell us what he wanted to sell because he did not have what we wanted.

It was too naïve to even think that I would have bought a Plasma television mistaking it to be an LCD. The approach of the store sales executive made me feel that he was making an attempt to short-change me. Probably he was not ... But my mind was made up. That was the last we saw of that store. We walked out promising never to return because it could not sustain our trust.

To be the owner of the Ferrari, it is important to gain people's trust. If you want to be valued, respected, trusted, understood, and followed, you must possess integrity of character. Winners, when confronted with tricky situations, just ask themselves one question—'What is right?' They answer this question honestly and then take decisions.

It is important to take the right stance at the very beginning. Once you take a morally incorrect stance, even if you retract and tread on the right path, the damage is done. People will never trust you in the same manner that they could have.

Let us take the example of a typical FMCG (Fast Moving Consumer Good) sales process. A Hindustan Lever sales executive dumps carton after carton of Lux soaps on a distributor with the promise that if he is not able to sell them, he will take them back and brand them as defective pieces. For the record ... he books a sale—a large one, at that, and he continues doing this month after month. In no time, the sales executive becomes a star salesperson. On the other hand, there is another salesperson who struggles to sell only half the number of cartons a month, but sells it the right way. Clearly, the performance of this person lags behind. After about eighteen months of such sales practices, the lid blows off the former salesperson's antics. Given the past performance the organisation is lenient towards this person and does not sack him. His sales volumes obviously drop from the previous high. However, the individual still sells more than the second executive.

Six months later, if an opportunity of giving one of them a larger role was to arise, who would the company give it to? If I was the decision maker, I would unhesitatingly give it to the second sales executive. If you ask, 'Why?', the answer is clear. As a supervisor, I would give leadership roles to an average resource high on integrity, rather than a brilliant resource with suspect integrity. Ideally, however, I would prefer an individual with integrity as well as high competence. But, if I am unable to find someone I would compromise on competence rather than on integrity.

The bottom line is, the Ferrari can be yours only if you are absolutely unwilling to compromise on integrity and ethics.

While maintaining the highest standard of ethics is important, it is also the key to manage your personal life without any blemishes. Often, ethical compromises in one's personal life, tend to reflect in your professional life as well.

The HR manager of an organisation I know of, was on the take, and would demand and take kickbacks from the recruitment consultants to hire candidates referred by them.

He was happily married to an ex-colleague of his. All was well between them until the HR manager began his perverse ways. He started having an affair with a girl from the training unit in the same organisation. Soon, his wife learnt of it and walked out on him and she sang like a canary about all his underhand dealings. The HR manager lost his job. Once she got to know, even his girlfriend left him. This is how a wayward personal life, low on integrity impacted a career.

Therefore, it is very important to maintain the highest degree of integrity. People form opinions about others and these opinions are often difficult to change. It takes only one move to create a negative impression, which stays for life.

Many a time, when you had to allocate a task at hand to a particular person, you must have felt, 'I won't give it to him, I'm not sure how honest he is.' Probably, you have not even worked with the person in question, but his behaviour drives you to form this opinion. Quite often, ideas are formed about individuals' professional behaviour and capabilities based on their personal etiquettes.

If you want to acquire the Ferrari, you cannot get to it alone. You need your team to work with you. And, how do you build a team? Do you know why dealing with your teammates with integrity and honesty is important? I was once told by Ajay Bimbhet, a stalwart in the banking industry, who I worked with for a very short period of time, that people work for organisations and people leave because of their supervisors. If you want to be successful, you need to get a great team of colleagues working for you. They will stay with you and work for you, only if they trust you.

If they get even an iota of doubt on your trustworthiness, you will cease being the boss. And if that happens even once, you will never be able to get that allegiance from your team, and without a cohesive and united team, you will never be able to come up with good performances. Post that, if you still have hopes of a Ferrari, you would have taken the positive thoughts concept as detailed in the previous chapter, to new heights.

COMMANDMENT FOUR

Set and follow the highest standard of integrity in your personal and professional lives. If you are high on integrity, people will respect and value you. The Ferrari when it comes, will stay with you.

Ten

Value Time

The erstwhile American President, John F. Kennedy once narrated an interesting story about the French Marshal Lyautey:

The great French Marshall Lyautey once asked his gardener to plant a tree. The gardener objected that the tree was slow growing and would not reach maturity for hundred years. The Marshall replied, "In that case, there is no time to lose; plant it this afternoon!"

This brings us to the scarcest and the most wasted commodity in this world—TIME. Time is invaluable, be it yours or others.

To get all there is out of living, we must employ our time wisely, never being in too much of a hurry to stop and sip life, but never losing our sense of the enormous value of a minute.

ANONYMOUS

Most people care little about this precious resource, procrastinate and leave everything for the last minute. I read a very interesting statement somewhere, a few days back. It said, 'Had it not been for the eleventh hour, most of the things in the world would be left incomplete'. How true!

Think as to what would happen if the last minute disappeared from your schedule. Look back to all the activities you did last week and see for yourself. Knock off the final minute from the activities you did the last week. The result is, almost everything is left unfinished, because you left everything for the eleventh hour. The obvious consequence is that your effectiveness suffers.

I remember a meeting I attended once. It was chaired by the new retail bank head of HSBC, Rajnish Bahl. The meeting was attended by all his direct reports. Rajnish had taken over, only a few weeks ago, and, therefore, there was a fair bit of suspense about the agenda for this meeting. We walked into the conference room, wondering what lay in store. HSBC's Indian business was to be hit by an audit in a fortnight, and everyone predicted that Rajnish would speak about it.

The meeting began on time; in fact, all meetings at HSBC begin on time. Punctuality is one aspect of doing business which I learnt at HSBC. Rajnish walked in and spoke to the team for over thirty minutes on his vision for the business and the shape he would like it to assume. This was the first time he was addressing the team and everyone was listening intently. Everybody was curious. Why was this meeting called? And, the answer came within the next five minutes.

'Friends, now that I've outlined my dream of the retail banking business for this bank; it's time to put some numbers on the table. We need to draw up a plan now which will become our bible for the next five years. All you business heads need to put your minds together and come up with the plan of your business for the next five years.' He then paused, partly for the effect and partly to gauge the reaction of the crowd. There was a flurry of activity in the room. Everyone looked at each other, a few papers crossed hands, and worried looks appeared on some faces. The confident ones looked at Rajnish and smiled. 'Yes, we should go for this exercise.'

'Okay,' continued Rajnish, 'we need to draw up a strategic five-year plan for all our businesses. Once that's done, we need to agree on an action plan and follow it. We must ensure that whatever is put in the strategic plan is achieved. Do you think we should be doing this at all?'

Everybody nodded.

'Sanjay will work with all of you on this. When do you think we can complete this exercise?'

There was a silence in the room.

'How much time do you require?'

Finally, someone spoke up, 'Rajnish, we have a group audit hitting us in the next two weeks. We all will be tied up with that. We can do this once the audit is over ... say, within a month.'

'Audit starts in fifteen days, it'll go on for another fifteen days and a month post that ... that makes it sixty days ... two months?'

'Yes, Rajnish.'

Rajnish shook his head in despair. 'Not good enough.'

'We can possibly do it fifteen days post the audit, that's forty-five days from now. However, let's not distract ourselves from the audit preparation,' someone spoke up. Rajnish was still shaking his head. He looked at Sanjay and grinned. What did he want? None of them knew. All they knew was that he was their new boss and a demanding one, at that. 'How does five days sound?' Rajnish asked.

'Rajnish, five days after audit is tough, but I guess we can finish it in about ten days after audit, if we do some preparatory work now and during the audit.' Another of his subordinates was out to please him. He looked at the others and smiled, his chest swelled up a few inches, thrilled that he was about to strike a deal.

'I am referring to five days from today!' That was a bombshell. There was a pin-drop silence in the room. Everyone turned their eyes towards Rajnish. What the heck! Had he lost it? Five days for drawing up a strategic plan for the next five years. Five days … ONLY!!

'Rajnish … audit … we have to prepare …'

'Team, none of you'd be directly involved in the audit. Your teams will be working on it. But that's not the reason why I'm giving you five days to complete the plan. Even if I give you sixty days to complete this, work will happen only on the last five days, from the fifty-fifth day to the sixtieth day. If you're anyway going to work on the plan only for five days, why wait for fifty-five days to begin. Let's start today and be done with it in the next five days. Gentlemen, this is non-negotiable. I've intimated to Sanjay what my expectations are from each of your businesses and he will coordinate with you. We will meet again on Saturday morning at 8.30 a.m. in the same room … with the five-year strategic plan.' And he walked out leaving no room for any discussion, leaving behind ten helpless souls wondering what had hit them. What happened after that was nothing short of a miracle. In the next five days the five-year strategic plan was delivered and even the audit preparations did not suffer. The organisation cleared the audit with flying colours.

If work can be prioritised and time managed effectively, everything is bound to fall on schedule. People who realise this are the ones who climb the ladder of success, and they do this quite fast because they value their time.

In the end, when Rajnish asked for prioritisation of the activity in question, despite people asking for sixty days, it got done in five days flat. Now, think of what you can achieve if you start doing this on your own.

If Rajnish had not prioritised and let the plan take its own course, audit would have come and gone in thirty days. Work on putting the strategic plan documents together, would have begun after the audit and it would have stretched for another thirty days, during which everything else would have come to a standstill. By doing what he did, Rajnish not only hastened the audit preparation by cutting on the available time but also saved thirty days post audit which were put to use for other productive work. He saved time not only for himself, but also for his team.

If you want to own the Ferrari, would you not want time to drive it around the town? What is the point in acquiring the Ferrari if it is parked in the garage all the time? You need to manage your time in such a manner that you get time to drive the Ferrari and show it to the world, as well.

There is an age-old proverb: *Work expands itself to completely fill in the available time.*

This speaks of poor time management by most people. And unfortunately, it is true. I read about a world class organisation which had over five thousand employees. It worked six days a week. A regular 'Voice of Employee' survey showed that employees believed that they were extremely stretched and had no time for themselves and their families—in other words, no 'work-life' balance. It was so serious that the management decided that they needed to shift to a five-day week. This would give the employees a two day break.

As a result, the organisation lost a day every week. But the CEO took a very interesting call. He said that for the next three months, the organisation would not hire anyone to supplement capacity, but would do it after three months, if required. It was expected that people would work longer hours for five days to take care of the loss of one working day. The CEO then started keeping records of the 'in' and 'out' timings of everyone without them knowing that they were being timed. An interesting finding emerged. There was no change whatsoever, in the time that people came in or left for home. The ones who were used to leaving at 6.30 p.m., left at the same time as before, the ones who stayed till 8.30 p.m. every day, stayed till 8.30 p.m. even now. Surprisingly, there was no drop in productivity of employees in these three months. The performance of the organisation, too, remained the same as before.

What does this indicate? The same employees, who cribbed about 'work-life' balance and work overload, now completed the same work that they took six days to finish, in five days. How could they, unless, earlier, they were wasting their time and not using it effectively, when they worked for six days? Alternately, if they could finish all their work in five days, why should they need to complain of excessive work when they were working for six days?

There was only one difference. Everyone started managing their time productively when they had to finish their work in five days. In the six-day scenario, work expanded to fill in the available time.

Managing time effectively can have a dramatic impact on your professional, social and personal lives. You would have definitely attended meetings with the senior management of your organisation? Have you ever been late for these meetings? Never, of course. Primarily, because you did not want your career and reputation to be at stake. Have you ever thought why this happens? Is this because senior management is extremely busy and does not have time to wait? The answer is a big NO. The correct answer to this question, however, is that people who are more successful and have risen up the career-graph and have achieved something in life, value their own time and even yours. They do not appreciate their schedules going haywire because of a delay by someone else. Have you seen successful people live their lives through their calendars?

They manage their time and meetings and tasks efficiently. If it is important, they jot it down on their calendar. If it does not find a mention there, it implies it is not important enough.

I am sure many of you have been to renowned doctors. They see fewer patients than their counterparts in government hospitals. However, the former category is very stringent about their clients keeping their appointments and coming in on time, whereas the latter does not care. Not only do they manage their time well, they also ensure that they meet you at the given time—remember the concept of valuing other's time as well. That is the reason why you begin to value and respect them, apart from competence, of course. That is how they become important, grow in their respective professions and become the rightful claimants of the Ferrari.

COMMANDMENT FIVE

Value your own time and that of the others, and be rest assured that the Ferrari will come to you.

Eleven

Strive for Perfection

Anusha, my daughter of seven, as any other girl of her age, loves to splash about in water and play in the pool with friends for hours. However, since she is yet to perfect her swimming skills, she remains within the baby pool. Whenever she feels like swimming in the larger pool, I pad up her arms with inflated floaters and she moves from one end of the pool to the other and back, beating furiously in the water, the floaters ensuring that she does not drown.

A few months back, she was to go on an excursion to a farmhouse in Lonavala. When my wife went to drop her off to the school bus, she got to know from the other parents that the farmhouse had a large pool and the school was organising a

> ***The fool doth think he is wise, but the wise man knows himself to be a fool.***
>
> WILLIAM SHAKESPEARE

game of water polo, too. Worried, Dharini turned towards Anusha, 'Promise me, you'll not jump into the water.'

'Why *amma*?' Anusha returned an innocent question.

'What do you mean ... why? What if the pool is deep?'

'Don't worry, *amma*. I know how to swim, I'll manage,' and she ran away to play with her other friends leaving Dharini in a state of shock.

What Dharini did after that was not at all surprising to me. She dragged Anusha away from there, put her in the car and returned home. Some of the teachers' phone numbers were retrieved and calls were made requesting Anusha to be excused from the trip. Anusha, as expected, was devastated. She cried the whole day. It took her four days to recover completely. Her friends at school kept telling her about all the fun they had and all that Anusha had missed, and this made her even more depressed.

However, if you ask me, Dharini did the right thing by bundling her in the car and bringing her back home. This prompts me to ask the question—why did Dharini do what she did? The answer is pretty simple. Anusha was extremely confident that she could manage herself in the pool because she knew swimming. The truth was, however, completely different. Anusha did not know how to swim. She had never entered the deeper end of a pool without wearing floaters to keep her afloat. She was in a position worse than someone who did not know how to swim and was aware that he could not swim. At least that person would ensure that he stays away from water. But this little devil, would have happily jumped into the deeper end of the pool, without realising the consequences. Dharini did not want to take any chance and pulled her back home.

The incident clearly shows that you take the first step towards doomsday if you think you are perfect, when you actually are not. Imagine, what would happen if Anusha had jumped into the deep end of the pool! The same thing will happen to you if you take on an activity or a task without enhancing your skills of delivering them. You will never be successful in what you set out to achieve. The worst you can probably do is to perceive the area of your weakness as your biggest strength. People often tend to make this mistake and falter in life. Visualise a scenario, where you think you know how to drive the Ferrari, (but actually you do not). You get into the Ferrari and try driving ... Vroooom ... Vroooom ... Crrrrassshhhhh ... that is what will eventually happen. Your hard-earned and treasured Ferrari will be a mangled junkyard. Of course, you would not allow this to happen. Would you?

If you want to continue driving your Ferrari on the road, you must keep pace with the changing traffic conditions. The world today is changing. What is 'in' today is 'out' tomorrow. People are changing, so are their needs and lifestyles. To be successful today, it is necessary to upgrade skills constantly, and also to make an effort at keeping abreast of the rapid changes around the world.

Sam Pitroda says: *Not only have the rules of the game changed, but the game itself has changed. While the rest of the world is playing baseball, developing nations cannot afford to play kabaddi.* The statement is thought provoking. When the world has gone ahead, if you do not imbibe in yourself the skills required for being successful in a changing environment, you will soon be extinct.

Take this simple example from the banking industry (I admit my bias for banking.) A bank branch is a place where the customer comes in to conduct normal banking transactions. A few years back, I was the branch manager of ANZ Grindlays Bank in Chennai. In those days banks were mainly deposit gatherers. The key responsibility of the branch manager was to get deposits from customers, to pursue them for more fixed deposit accounts. This was the scenario in the mid to late nineties.

And then, the mutual fund wave hit the financial service industry. Banks moved from being deposit gatherers to the sellers of mutual funds and other investment products. Anyone who did not know about mutual funds suddenly found himself unfit to be in the branch environment. Employees were trained and equipped with the respective skill-sets to start the selling of mutual funds. Those who did not make an effort to learn were left behind. In no time, insurance made its presence felt. The branches started selling insurance products, and then came all the loan products. Over a period of time, bank branches were modified from being a deposit gathering unit to a supermarket for all financial products. This posed a challenge for the bank employees in the late nineties. The expectations from them changed. And, to deliver on the changed set of expectations, they had to either acquire new skill-sets, or move out of a branch.

What would have possibly happened to a branch manager of the late nineties, who refused to change and upgrade his skill-sets? From a 'star manager', he would have crashed down to the lowest rung of performers in the branch league tables.

The message from this example, as well as from Sam Pitroda's quote, is that the only thing which is constant in this world is change. Either embrace change and prepare yourself for it or perish, the choice is yours. The only way out is to anticipate change and acquire the skill-sets necessary to deal with it.

If you aspire for the Ferrari, you will have to get out of your comfort zones and learn the skill-sets necessary for this day and age. It is a constantly changing world and what is good today, may not be good tomorrow, what is 'perfect' today may be a gross misfit tomorrow. But, learning is not dealing with change alone. It is about equipping yourself with the edge which drives you so much ahead of your competitors that they will take a long time pacing up to you. Learning helps you deal with your aspirations, go after them and make them a reality.

The secret key to the Ferrari lies in accepting that no one is perfect. But you can STRIVE TO BE PERFECT through an elaborate and logical learning process. The moment an individual believes that he or she is perfect, learning stops. And when learning stops, fall from grace is imminent. The secret of the Ferrari lies in accepting the fact that one is not perfect and keep working towards achieving it in this perpetually evolving world.

Aim at perfection in everything, though in most things it is unattainable. However, they who aim at it, and persevere, will come much nearer to it than those whose laziness and despondency make them give it up as unattainable.

LORD CHESTERFIELD

Those who think they are perfect are heading for a disaster, for a fall so great that he will never be able to recover.

Successful people, the Ferrari owners, are those who are able to anticipate the change or more importantly, participate in driving change. This change could be in the environment, in the place of work, at home or even in themselves. This helps them, because if they drive the change then they are better prepared to deal with it. Individuals, who aspire for the Ferrari, do not wait for others to help them learn, they do not wait for others to tell them to learn, to come close to perfection ... they tell others that it is time they moved on.

Many of you definitely would have heard of Laurie Lawrence, the former Australian Rugby Union representative and an Olympic and world champion swimming trainer. He has represented Australia in world championships, Commonwealth Games and Olympic Games as a coach. His protégés included many champion swimmers as Duncan Armstrong (1988 Seoul Olympics), Jon Seiben (1984 Los Angeles Olympics), Steve Holland and also Tracy Wickham, who is regarded as one of Australia's greatest women swimmers. Laurie has retired from being an active swimming trainer, but has been retained by the Australian team as a motivational coach for the Beijing Olympics in 2008.

I was fortunate enough to interact with Laurie when he had come to deliver a motivational speech to a team of champions from my organisation in Singapore. He told us a very interesting story about the 'Australian Swimming Sensation', Ian Thorpe and his coach Doug Frost. Thorpe was just eight years old when Frost spotted him, steered him to become the youngest male swimmer to represent Australia and win a world title. The year was 1988, when Ian Thorpe captured the 400 metres freestyle. Since then, Thorpe has taken the world of swimming by storm and has won five golds in Olympic Games, eleven world titles and established thirteen different world records ... something which no one had ever done before.

At the 2002 Commonwealth Games, Thorpe won six golds and broke his own 400 metres freestyle world record. Anyone else would have been ecstatic at this performance. Sadly, Thorpe was not. He took a decision. This decision was to shake the world of swimming.

In September 2002, Thorpe dropped a bombshell. He was leaving his coach. Doug Frost, his coach for over thirteen years, had been honoured as Australia's 'Coach of the Year' for the last two consecutive years. And, Thorpe was leaving him. The entire swimming fraternity was up in arms. Even more stunning was what Thorpe followed it up with. He announced that Tracey Menezies, a twenty-nine-year-old art teacher at East Hill Boys High, Thorpe's former school, and his former 'learn to swim' coach would be his new trainer and coach. What made it even worse was that Tracey part-timed as an assistant coach with Doug Frost.

Laurie Lawrence was closely associated with both Frost and Thorpe. He, like everyone else, was also extremely annoyed with Thorpe's decision. Though he tried calling Thorpe a couple of times, he was unable to get through. Laurie was itching to ask him why he did, what he did.

As luck would have it, he met Thorpe on a flight to Melbourne, where he was going for a presentation. They were sitting next to each other. He had to ask him now. 'Thorpe,' he said, 'tell me honestly, why did you leave Doug for that woman?' At that point Frost was the best coach in Australia and there was no one of his stature. Thorpe gave him a bemused look.

'Laurie, I love Doug Frost. I appreciate everything Doug's done for me. I owe almost everything that I've today to him. He taught me to swim, he was the one responsible for my high-elbow style, he fine-tuned my big-foot swimming ... I owe everything to him.'

'The world knows this Thorpe ... then why?'

'Because had I not left my coach, I would definitely have been out of swimming before the next Olympics.'

Laurie did not understand a word. He just shook his head in despair.

'Laurie, as a young swimmer, I had lots of ideas, lots of thoughts on how to change and improve the way I swim. I wanted to try out new things. But as I grew older, Doug didn't let me expand. Everyday at training, Doug would come up and say, "Thorpe ten 400s." I would try and tell him, "Doug can we ...?" Doug used to retort, "I said ten 400s ... do as I say. I am the coach," and then I'd jump into the pool and start doing those laps. I'd gotten to such a stage that I was beginning to hate the sport. He didn't allow me to grow. I felt stifled. I was looking for a coach who'd help me in my pursuit of excellence in swimming and not with respect to the current crop of competition. Doug was preparing me for today, I wanted to be ready for tomorrow.'

That was when Laurie told us, 'If a man like Thorpe, who has attained such high levels of success in life in that one sport, was feeling stifled and was even thinking of quitting the sport because he wasn't learning anything new, not getting closer to perfection, think of moderate achievers, think of the whole lot of people who work across levels in various organisations. Shouldn't they be feeling even worse?'

Winners love challenge and they love to take up new and arduous tasks. Routine bores them, they always seek to explore something new. Winners are those who are curious to learn more, even if it means walking off the beaten track. In Thorpe's case, he was no longer challenged by his immediate competitors. He had achieved more than what anyone could imagine. He wanted to face greater challenge ... to compete with himself. Frost had nothing new to offer him. So, he ventured out in his quest for knowledge. He is the true owner of the Ferrari.

The message that Laurie left us and the one I am sharing with you is very clear. If you want to grow in life, it is important to constantly innovate and learn new ways of doing things; in other words, it is extremely important to enrich your skill-sets by constant learning and development. It is critical to expand your capabilities in order to keep winning and be on the top. If you do not do it, you will feel suffocated, stifled, and monotonous and this is the root cause for negative thoughts creeping into your minds. And, I have already spoken about the necessity of your mind to be clouded by positive thoughts, if you want to own the Ferrari.

> *Only the curious will learn and only the resolute overcome the obstacles to learning. The quest quotient has always excited me more than the intelligence quotient.*
>
> EUGENE WILSON

If you want to survive in this competitive world, you cannot stand still. You will have to pace up with the others and constantly learn while you run. Else, your skill-sets will be overtaken by someone else and the Ferrari will stay as elusive as ever.

COMMANDMENT SIX

No one is perfect. The moment you think you are, it is the countdown to doomsday. Earning the Ferrari is all about constantly upgrading yourself, improving your skill-sets and equipping yourself for the future. And for this, the initiative has to be yours.

Twelve

Befriend Achievers

I was discussing success with a few of my friends the other day and interesting definitions came up in the process.

One said, 'Success is another name for career enhancement.'

'Success is money. Wealth creation is the ultimate measure of success!!!' argued another.

'Fame, maybe. That's what Bollywood stars get.'

'Well, no. It's about the difference you make to mankind.'

We debated for hours but could not reach a consensus. How could we? After all, intelligent minds always stay in a state of positive conflict.

The greenest bush will always be found on the periphery of a well manured field.
ANONYMOUS

The definition of success actually depends on where you

look for it. And, if you speak to ten different individuals, you are likely to get ten different perspectives. Philosophy and religion will define success as the impact you make on mankind, the suffering you alleviate from this society and will define success for corporate professionals as CSR (Corporate Social Responsibility).

But, if you ask a youngster of today, the answer will be completely different. For them money, career and fame—constitute the scale on which success is measured. There is nothing wrong in it. If that is where the world is leading to, it is necessary to adhere to it.

Once you have developed your own definition of success, you need to associate with people who have reached the pinnacles in the field of your interest, so, BEFRIEND ACHIEVERS. There are a number of ways in which you can approach the leaders and learn from them. I will tell you of the golden rules for this.

Be in the Immediate Company of the Winners

If you work with Fiat Group, the chances of driving around in a Ferrari are definitely higher for you. Tagging along with the achievers may not be the only way to achieve success, but it definitely is a potent way. Many people do not publicly subscribe to this manner of growth but you will have to take my word, when I say that this is probably the most common means of growth in today's corporate world.

Join Winning Organisations and Teams

This is a long-term approach, wherein you join corporate houses and organisations whose leadership is renowned. These organisations are not only leaders in their respective fields of operation but also believe in developing individuals into centres of excellence. If you become a part of these kinds of organisations, you yourself will achieve wealth and fame by virtue of being associated with them. You join, not for immediate gains but for developing yourself, for learning, for building your own brand equity so that you give yourself an edge over the others.

This is not only true of organisations but also individuals in power and rank. Have you observed what happens whenever new CEOs take up their responsibilities? All the employees who are to report to the new bosses in their respective organisations live on tenterhooks for days at a stretch. They are often uncertain about retaining their jobs. Why?

Because, whenever new successors come in the top management positions, they drag along their own sets of loyal subordinates. This happens all the time in every industry. In my limited career, I have seen this happen several times, when people have shifted jobs, changed careers, tagging along with one individual and moving lock, stock and barrel with him.

Why does this happen? Well, primarily because it suits both sides of the coin. At senior levels, people generally prefer to work with colleagues they are comfortable with. When new CEOs take over in organisations, they would prefer to bring in their own teams, their allies, the colleagues with whom they have worked in the past ... people whom they trust.

On the other hand, those who move along with such seniors, do so because of two reasons: First, they have faith in the capability of the leaders they follow. They tag along with these people believing that they will emerge successful by working under their superiors. Second, they are opportunists, who see some immediate gains in following their superiors.

More often, it is the former of the above two reasons which lead you to the Ferrari. Successful people, build teams, work cohesively, and build dreams and businesses together. Togetherness and trust enable them to achieve impossible missions. An immediate example which comes to my mind is of Tony Singh.

Tony Singh started his career at American Express where he worked for over fifteen years, before he joined as the retail bank head with Bank of America. At Bank of America, he was instrumental in growing the retail business chain. When the bank decided to exit the retail business, he negotiated the sale of their business to ABN Amro in India, wherein he negotiated a great financial deal for the Bank of America staff. At Bank of America he had created his own team, a team of achievers, a team of believers and those who had faith in him. This team was the core retail banking team at Bank of America. The team split when ABN bought over Bank of America.

From ABN, Tony Singh joined ANZ Grindlays Bank as the CEO, and the entire team regrouped. They changed the face of ANZ Grindlays Bank in India, transforming it into a world class enterprise, prior to it getting sold to Standard Chartered Bank. Once this was done, Tony Singh moved on to Max New York Life as the CEO and the same team joined him there, helping him set up that business. As the team moved from Bank of America, to ANZ to Max New York Life, each one of the team members gained in stature, exposure, capability and of course, financially, too ... all this on account of their association with the leader, Tony Singh. They are much closer to the Ferrari now than they ever were.

There is a small caveat here. Your wanting to join a team is not the only pre-requisite for you to get into a Ferrari team. The leaders or the people you wish to associate yourself with, need to perceive you as a performer with a like mindset. And, also you must demonstrate an aligned approach with these leaders. You need to bring some value to their table.

While Tony Singh's example is at the upper end of the spectrum, you see this happening in your everyday life. In fact, you will often see people aligning their careers with individuals in your organisation every day. This comes out in the open when people leave organisations. Along with a senior resignation you will see a host of others resigning ... some of them are genuine believers who follow the leader and others are opportunists who follow in search of the gold.

There is no need to go even that far, within large organisations when senior employees moving from one unit to the other, move with their entire entourage. Their favourites follow them even within the same organisation and the seniors happily oblige.

Remember, a mediocre guy with a brilliant boss gets noticed whereas a brilliant guy with a mediocre boss in a not so successful unit often fails to make the cut. Hence, there is nothing wrong in tagging along with the successful boss to further the desire of getting the Ferrari.

What are the risks associated with this method of chasing the Ferrari? There is one pronounced one.

Successful people will always have adversaries. There are

colleagues who may challenge their achievements. By attaching yourself to Mr A, who does not get along with Mr B, you are in effect shutting out any opportunity that may spring up with Mr B. If ever a situation were to arise wherein you have to leave the confines of the secure environment provided by Mr A, you will face some resistance within your own organisation. But at times the benefits of this modus operandi far exceed the downsides and, therefore, it is definitely worth an effort.

The bottom line is, aligning yourself with high performing individuals and backing yourself with reasonably high performance level will take you a few notches closer to the Ferrari.

COMMANDMENT SEVEN

Identify the owners of the Ferrari and align yourself with them.

If you are in the company of successful people, their success will rub off on you. But you need to back it up with stellar performance. If you live in Ferrari town, chances are, you will get to drive one sooner.

Thirteen

Share the Success

Indians are generally god-fearing and religious.Every religion across the length and breadth of this country promotes the concept of giving. Take Hinduism for instance, according to dharma, everyone is required to give dana (donation) and the seva(service). Hindus are expected to make donations to the poor as well as to their places of worship. Hinduism even goes on to elaborate that if you SHARE what you have with others, you will get back much more than that. It may not always come back to you from the same person you helped, but will definitely come back in this life.

> *If you light a light for somebody, it will also brighten your path.*
>
> BUDDHIST PROVERB

Indians by their sheer nature feel for others' needs and wants. In an Indian society more than anywhere else, the importance of giving and sharing is paramount.

Speaking of the principle of what you give comes back to you, I would add an anecdote here about Sir Alexander Fleming, which reconfirms this paradigm.

Fleming's father once saved a rich Scottish farmer's child from drowning in quicksand. The farmer was extremely thankful to Fleming's father. And as a mark of gratitude, he offered to support Fleming's education. In due course of time the young Fleming grew up, and became a great scientist, and consequently discovered Penicillin. And, when the farmer's son was suffering from pneumonia, Penicillin cured him. The moral is, good deeds done always return to the doer. And, that was what happened, first in the case of Fleming's father and then the farmer.

Narayana Murthy, the chief mentor of Infosys, says: *For Heavens sake, there is nothing wrong in creating wealth by legal and ethical means. Do not ever confuse creation of wealth with charity. First, you create wealth efficiently and only then can you donate your share of profit to any charity. If you don't earn, what will you give.*

There can be no two opinions on what Narayana Murthy says. If you want to give your needy neighbour a ride, you must have the Ferrari first. To share your wealth with others, you need to create wealth first. And, once you have generated wealth, you must use a part of it, in some way or the other, for social well being.

If you step back and take a look at the owners of the Ferrari, the common thing bound to cross your mind is their commitment to the overall upliftment of the society. Most of them share their success with others—be it in the form of educational support to the poor, or providing food for them, or donating to various intermediary NGOs ... they do it all. Sharing a part of the wealth by no means diminishes it. A ride that you give your neighbour does not diminish the worth of a Ferrari. Does it?

Coming back to Infosys, Nandan Nilekani, one of the founder members of Infosys, is very clear on his intent to make a difference to the society outside the Infosys campus. He earns in crores every year but also spends crores on the upliftment of the society. In fact, when he and his wife Rohini, made their first hundred crores from the Infosys ADR (American Depository Receipts) issue, she donated almost the entire amount to an educational foundation she runs. Nandan believes, the more he earns, greater the responsibility on him to pass some of it back to the society that helped him get it. Moreover, he argues that he does not need so much money to fulfil his needs. Therefore, rather than let it rot in a bank, he prefers to plough it back into the society.

However, you do not need to become a Nandan Nilekani to give others a ride in the Ferrari. You can make a difference within your means.

To make the impact felt, all you need to do is to give it a try.

My last supervisor was a British gentleman. He would participate in the Mumbai Marathon every year, with only one aim—raising funds for charity, for a cause that he supported. By promising to run the marathon for charity, he would raise money from various people he knew within and outside the organisation he worked for. He would promise them two things. First, he would match any contribution that they would make. Second, he would run the marathon for the cause and at the end of the race, would hand over the cheque of the entire amount to the NGO he supported. The NGO website confirms him as the single largest individual fundraiser for them.

> ***If you think you are too small to make a difference, try spending a night in a closed room with a solitary mosquito.***
> ANONYMOUS

The reason behind doing this is simple—most of the successful people are the ones who have come up the hard way. And now that they are successful, they wish to do their bit for the society they grew up in. Be it Bill Gates and Melinda Gates' Foundation, or Sudha and Narayana Murthy's Foundation, people who are successful make it a point to share their Ferrari with others who have not acquired one.

So, if you earn, you give. On a spiritual note, it is said that if you share what you have with others, if you work on the upliftment of the downtrodden, if you work towards the achievement of a social cause and set aside a part of your earnings towards this, the blessings of those people will not go to waste. All those blessings will have an impact and will come back to make you a very successful human being.... And, as we say—closer to the Ferrari.

COMMANDMENT EIGHT

Share your success with others. If you commit to uplift the down-trodden, you will become the true owner of the Ferrari.

Fourteen

Watch Out on Health

Now, I will tell my readers a story. No, neither have I gone crazy, nor we are here for café gossip. This fable, I heard in my childhood, helped me learn my lesson and I hope, it will have its bearing on you too.

In a forest, somewhere in southern Rajasthan, lived an arrogant lion. The lion was lazy, but a lion, nevertheless. Every animal was afraid of him and he ruled over the entire jungle. One day, he called all the animals. 'Listen,' he began, 'everyday, I chase and catch you folks to satiate my hunger. Why do you want to go through this trouble?'

> *Time and health are two precious assets that we don't recognise and appreciate until they have been depleted.*
>
> DENIS WAITLEY

'Great!!! So, you are going to spare us?' asked the monkey sitting on a treetop.

'No, you idiot!!' roared the lion. 'From today onwards, I want you all to decide among yourself and send me one animal every day. If you do that I will not kill any other animal.'

All the animals deliberated for sometime and agreed to the lion's proposal. Every day, they would send him one animal. This continued for few years. The animals were too scared of the lion and did not dare to fight the king. One day, a small dog went to the lion as his meal. When the dog entered the den, he found the lion sitting at the far end.

'Come here. I am hungry,' roared the lion. The dog was too scared to obey his orders. He stood at the entrance of the den. The lion roared and tried to scare the dog, but when the dog did not move towards him, the lion got up slowly and walked towards the dog. Huddled in the corner was the dog, waiting for his death, when suddenly he heard a loud crash. The lion had tripped over a protruding rock and had fallen down. He seemed to be in terrible pain. The dog waited for some time staring at the lion, thinking whether to go and help the lion, or flee from the ailing lion. When the lion did not get up for some time, the dog hit upon an idea. He ran back to all the animals and told them about it. In no time, all the animals got together and rushed to the den. The lion was still writhing in tremendous pain. The animals saw this as an opportunity, pounced on the lion and killed him. His laziness made him weak and unfit, thus, the opportunists struck when he was incapacitated.

Laziness makes even the most powerful creature vulnerable. So, it is at best avoided.

This is so true in life as well. How many of you want to associate yourselves with weak and unfit leaders? Those of us who want the Ferrari would want to link ourselves with people who can get there, who can help us on our way to the Ferrari, and not those who need our support to keep them afloat.

If you will not back leaders who are unfit, what makes you think that anyone else will back you if you are not fit. Leaders who are unfit or need regular props will not be able to get together a cohesive, single-minded team. And, if that does not happen, their chances of succeeding rapidly diminish. Without your team rallying behind you, it is unlikely that you are going to get any closer to the Ferrari.

Therefore, the lesson of this story is profound. All Ferrari owners live a HEALTHY and ACTIVE life. They do not allow their physical fitness to rust away. Be it famous political leaders, professionals, millionaire entrepreneurs, corporate chieftains, sportspersons, successful film stars ... all are fitness freaks.

Have you ever tried to jog for about three or four kilometres in the morning? It is not an easy thing to do. Have you ever followed the Annual Mumbai Marathon and tried to figure out who all participate in it? If you did, then you would know that the who's who of Mumbai come out on the streets to participate in it. And, if you are not one of those fitness freaks, you would also know that, leave alone running the entire distance of the marathon, jogging for a kilometre itself would not be possible. Then, how do these business and corporate chieftains manage it?

It is a kind of Catch. 22 paradox as to why successful individuals keep themselves fit. Since they are required to work long hours you may think that they can hardly manage to spare time for exercise. The point to note is that it is precisely because of this reason that they need to stay fit. They need to be in peak health so that they are able to concentrate on their work and deliver results. In fact, truly successful people never compromise on their fitness. They do not get time but they find time to exercise. Because they know that fitness is the key to productive output. To carry out the responsibilities of large organisations, big businesses and also a large number of employees who work with them and for them, they need to remain healthy. This is a lot of weight to carry. And, if you aspire to carry that weight at some point in time, must you not be fit enough to carry it?

In today's hectic work schedule, high workload, and competition, it is difficult to put a check on the stress level. With a sedentary lifestyle, poor food habits, excessive travel, and alcohol thrice a week you can hardly blame your body for revolting. The obvious consequences are heart and liver ailments and other stress disorders. Imagine a situation wherein you are out of work for a period of three months on account of a serious illness. Remember, if you are competing for the Ferrari, there will be five other opponents breathing on your shoulder, hoping that you topple, so that they can further their careers. Your prolonged absence from work, gives them an opportunity to wedge their way in. And, you would not want them to do that. Therefore, the higher your energy level, the more efficient your body. The more efficient your body, the better you feel and the more you will use your talent to produce outstanding results.

Ever heard of the term 'rat race'? Yes, life is indeed a race. And in this race, you cannot afford to go slow. You either run fast and stay ahead of the pack, or your competitors will overtake you. You can neither take a break, nor reduce steam. If you do slow down, you will be branded incompetent. And, once you are branded incompetent, it lasts forever. It becomes very difficult to enter the race again. So, run you must … and that too, hard ... and to run, you need strength, stamina and speed ... and for that you need to be fit.

COMMANDMENT NINE

Remain fighting fit and be in perfect shape. No one will entrust you with the Ferrari if you are not fit enough to drive it.
Work hard, exercise harder, build stamina, and keep illness at bay.
This is a sure shot way of getting into the driver's seat.

Fifteen

Build a Mind-boggling Profile

Success is a pedestal resting on two basic pillars—ACHIEVEMENTS and PERCEPTIONS of those achievements by the rest of the world.

If you have earned the Ferrari you would obviously want to drive it proudly along the town's busiest streets. Would you not want to show the world that you are its proud owner? This is what we all struggle and work hard for. Likewise, every successful person desires to be perceived as successful.

> *Good work not advertised is akin to kissing a girl in the dark. You don't know who you kissed, neither does the one you kissed.*
>
> ANONYMOUS

Achievement is quantifiable and measurable, perception is not. Achievements are actual deliverables, which to a large extent, are tangible. They are there for everyone to see and measure. You can control your achievements. They are normally in black and white and are often not open to individual interpretations.

However, where many individuals falter is in the latter, i.e. in managing the perceptions. They often have achievements to talk about, but fail in managing perceptions where it matters. As a result, their successes, their achievements go unnoticed and unrecognised. Let me explain how.

In any organisation, or even if you are running your own business, it is in your own interest that as many people as possible know about your achievements, even if they are not related directly or indirectly to your field of operation.

I knew a man who joined a foreign bank in Bangalore in 1995 as a relationship manager. In those days, relationship managers were responsible for acquiring new clients for the bank, primarily deposit holders. This gentleman brought in a twenty crores' deposit deal within sixty days of joining the bank—partly luck, partly persistence —but nothing that he did to get the deposit was extraordinary. This was at a time when the entire bank's deposit base in Bangalore was less than hundred crores. The Bangalore branch of this bank suddenly came into the limelight. The twenty-crore deposit deal became the talk of the bank. Victory messages flew thick and fast—there was no intranet in those days, else it would have been on that, too. Over the next few weeks, the deal was discussed again and again, over lunch, over dinner, in the elevator, in the pantry, in the wash room, and in every conceivable corner of the bank. This gentleman was hailed a hero.

A halo was created around him and that helped him get plum positions, quick jumps in his career, as a result, today he is a very successful banker. People who knew him in his twenty-crore days, are all over the banking industry and in very senior controlling positions in most of the foreign banks. They are the ones who have helped him grow in his career. Today, he heads a large business and is way ahead of his contemporaries in the way his career has moved. He is closer to the Ferrari than any of his contemporaries.

I met him some time back and casually asked him about the turning point in his career. As expected, he spoke of the twenty-crore deposit deal and all that followed suit.

'After that success,' he said, 'everyone started viewing me as a hotshot sales person. Today, if any of the seniors who were in the bank at that time, need a business head, they think of me and I owe this to the profile that my supervisor built for me after the twenty-crore deal.' If his boss had not publicised his success, no one would have known and he would have had to work harder to get noticed. It was the 'perception' that his supervisor instigated others to have about him that helped him climb up the career ladder.

Ever wondered why those at head offices, get their promotions faster than those at the branch offices? Why they get international assignments at a rapidity which is hardly seen at the branches? It is all about being noticed and performance getting its deserved recognition. I am not arguing whether this is right or wrong. All I am trying to say is that perception matters most!!!

There was this gentleman who joined a large MNC bank as a marketing head for India in the year 1996. In the last ten years he has risen from this position in India to one of the topmost positions globally. He is among the top-four executives in this global banking giant and is tipped to be one of the contenders for the next global CEO. And, how did this happen?

When a senior team came for visiting India, within eight months of his joining the bank, he was asked to make a presentation to the delegation, in the absence of his immediate boss. He made such a stunning presentation that everyone around was impressed, and within no time he was plucked out of the Indian operations and moved overseas. And, he has never looked back. Had he not got noticed on that day (and had he not made an effort to get noticed) would he have been even remotely close to where he is today. The answer is an obvious 'No', notwithstanding the fact that he was one of the brightest individuals to have worked for the bank in question.

Some people are fortunate enough to have supervisors who work on building profiles for them, exposing their talents to the top management, to the influencers. Some may not be as fortunate so they have to work on it themselves, but work they must to ensure that people talk of their accomplishments.

Whatever may be the case, the greatest benefit of building a good profile for yourself, even among unrelated people is that tomorrow if an opportunity arises, people will remember you. There may be others in the system who have delivered better than you have, but you will triumph because your profile will make you 'top of mind' recall. After a certain level in any organisation, profile and perceptions drive you closer to the Ferrari. That's because, beyond a certain level it is taken for granted that since you have reached this far, you have the capability to deliver. Given this assumption, the only thing which differentiates you from another performer is profile ... perception, i.e. how people see you. Public opinion in your favour definitely helps in your quest of the Ferrari.

At Citibank, for instance, promotions happen through a management committee debate, at specific times of the year. Generally, a list of all eligible candidates is drawn up and circulated among the members of the committee. Then on an agreed date and time, the entire management committee gets onto a conference call and talks through the entire list. The merits and demerits of promoting a particular individual is debated threadbare. The candidate's supervisor, who has observed him from close quarters often takes the lead and tries to push the promotion of his subordinate. In such a situation, just imagine the benefit that accrues to the candidate, if three more members on the management committee say, 'Yes, I know him. He is a wonderful resource and we must promote such a talent.' It makes his promotion air-tight. Often such comments from other uninvolved people make and mar the career prospects of individuals in corporate world. And, how do you ensure that three others in the management committee stand up and fight your cause? BUILD A PROFILE with everyone you think is important in your organisation.

As your depth of work in the company increases, you will know that loose comments about individuals can ring the death-knell for budding careers and casual positive comments from people not particularly completely informed can work wonders for your career.

In order to let others know your achievements, take the help of emails, and intranet (if your company has one), hone your networking skills, hunt down people in your organisation who, you are aware, will spread the word about what you have done. Avoid conflicts with influential people. If you have done something good, something different, something which you feel everyone in the organisation should know, go ahead and tell them. These are the same set of people who will help you on your way up the hill, on your way to the Ferrari.

Surely, building a profile without performance to back it up is not going to get you anywhere. But if you are a performer without the profile-building skills ... well, schedule visits to the nearest temple all seven days of the week ... You will need God Himself to come and help you in your quest for the Ferrari.

COMMANDMENT TEN

If you have followed all the commandments with dedication and determination, it is the time to build up a profile for yourself. Target your audience and announce your achievements. You will own the Ferrari in no time.

What Is The Ferrari?

Sixteen

The Ferrari Unwrapped

All through the book, I have been speaking about the Ferrari. I have also formulated Ten Commandments for acquiring the Ferrari. Readers must be wondering whether I am totally out of my wits to ramble over a mere four-wheeler manufactured by the Fiat Group. Well, I am not. The Ferrari I spoke of here is not just a car.

The Ferrari stands for:

Fortune for
Every
Right
Rigorous
And
Resourceful
Individual

Fortune

Fortune means success, fame, respect, social status, money, career, happiness and everything else that you associate with the winners. However, this word may have different implications for different people. Some of you may value fame more than wealth, while others may regard social status as the most important criterion. Whatever be the case, fortune here refers to that particular aspect of success which you value the most.

Right Individual

The Right Individual is honest, treads along the path of integrity even if it is not the easiest path. High on morals and values, this individual will never compromise on them even if it bears high cost.

Integrity in personal and professional life, being honest to the self and honest and fair with others is a trait which is often difficult to get, but so is the Ferrari. Maintaining high standards of integrity is the key to acquiring a Ferrari.

Rigorous Individual

This individual is totally focused on the goals—he aims for the peak and leaves no stone unturned to reach there. Setting high standards, making difficult decisions in the nick of time, working the guts out, here is a person, who does not shy away from burning the midnight oil in the mission to succeed. Always on the lead, following all the Ten Commandments, such a person never compromises on one thing, i.e. hard work.

Resourceful Individual

Dreaming and aspiring high and at the same time, backing himself up to transform them in reality, this individual is resourceful enough to realise his strengths and weaknesses and play with the strengths while working on the weaknesses. Such a person understands the value of time and deftly manages it. At the workplace, he tracks and tags on to successful people, to grow faster in life ... of course, with ingenious skills as well.

These are quite simple words, yet they carry a deeper meaning, which marks the dividing line between success and failure, between owning a Ferrari and ogling at one.

So simply put, acquiring the Ferrari means being successful in a particular field. Being one of a kind in whatever you do. Achieving name, fame, fortune, reputation and winning accolades. Whichever way you define success, achieving it is akin to acquiring the Ferrari.

Earlier in the book I mentioned the Ten Commandments for acquiring the Ferrari. If you read the four key words above and then revisit the Ten Commandments, you would see that each of those rules would fit into one of the three R's—Right, Rigorous and Resourceful.

A word of caution here. All the Ten Commandments are extremely critical in your quest for the Ferrari. Bear in mind that if you want to end up achieving what you aspire and dream, if you want to own the Ferrari, you must follow each one of the Ten Commandments. You cannot miss out on one, or be slack on the other. Adherence to these has to be complete—without exception, without excuse, because there is no part-ownership of the Ferrari. It is either complete ownership, or no ownership at all. Similarly, you are either a success or a failure, you cannot dangle in between.

As is obvious now and as the owners of Ferraris would bear me out, the Ferrari does not come easy. The Ferrari is always perched on top of the hill and it is a daunting task to get there. The path round the hill may be winding and long. You might often stumble, yet you must walk on. Hurdles will come and go. Sacrifices have to be made. Only the best of the best get there. You need to be determined enough. If you are one of those committed ones who make it ... there shines the bright red immaculate Ferrari, all for you. Make it your own. Acquire one for yourself.

Once you get it into your garage, cherish the Ferrari. Show it off to the entire world that you have one. It is a rare occurrence. You are one of the deserving few. Keep it that way.

This brings me to the next point. Do not be defensive about owning the Ferrari. It is something to be proud of. There are numerous people, who do not own one, but aspire for it. It is a scarce commodity and you are no undeserving person to have achieved it. So, flaunt your Ferrari. Wear it on your sleeve.

In your quest for the Ferrari, it is possible to be tempered by millions of people on the face of this earth, who will tell you that a Ferrari is just not worth it. 'It comes at a price … a high price,' they will say.

What is the 'price' that these people talk of? They refer to things like, very little time left to pursue alternate interests, high mental and emotional stress, and little or no time for the family, etc. I beg to disagree. Escapists, I would call all of them.

You have to realise one thing that the Ferrari is not owned by millions. It is only for the crème de la crème. As it is, winners are few in number … even fewer among them own the Ferrari. So, all these comments coming from all around you are nothing but ridiculous excuses made up by the millions who do not even get a glimpse of a Ferrari, let alone acquiring one.

So, my message to everyone who has reached thus far is, folks, stay focused, follow the Ten Commandments and you will own the Ferrari one day. No one can detract you from your mission. No one can stop the Ferrari from becoming yours.

Going back to where we began our story, to Julian Mantle, the young lawyer in Robin Sharma's *The Monk Who Sold His Ferrari*—the lawyer, who sells his mansion, his private island, his jetplane, even his prized Ferrari and goes off to the mountains, where he meets Yogi Raman in the magical land of Sivana. The yogi teaches him the secrets of leading a successful, contended and uncomplicated life. The yogi is his divine inspiration, who helps him acquire traits which would in turn make him an extremely successful individual. The yogi tells him to follow a vision, develop positive thoughts, experience the joys of sharing, and hard work. The hotshot lawyer, after experiencing his days of nirvana returns to his land, a wise man, and begins to lead a peaceful and blissful life.

But hey, hold on! These are the very traits that you require to acquire the Ferrari. If you revisit the Ten Commandments, you will realise that they are quite the same ones that the Yogi eventually teaches the young lawyer. And Julian, for that matter, never sold off his Ferrari, in the true sense. He just bartered a four-wheeler in exchange of insights and lessons that would gain him the FERRARI – Fortune for Every Right, Rigorous and Resourceful Individual. This FERRARI is something which he would never fathom selling or getting rid of. Anyone who gets to the pinnacle and acquires one, knows how rare it is. And if Julian ever happens to sell off this FERRARI, ... I would make him a final requisition ... let me know ... I will buy it!!!

Ferrari, Ferrari, where are you?
Ferrari, Ferrari, I aspire for you.
With so few around, so many in queue,
I will claw my way to get my due.

There is only one reason for my existence,
Aren't you the genesis of my persistence!!
One look at you, everything I do, starts making sense,
I want you ... I will make no pretence.

Hard work and integrity will get me there,
Negative thoughts dispelled, I have no fear.
'I am perfect—a foolish illusion,
Strife to improve will chase off the delusion.

The day you come to me, I'll drive you round town,

To hell with the envious detractors' frowns.
On my Ferrari, I will give a ride to the needy,
Will share with the society, I shall not be greedy.

Ten Commandments will I follow, always as usual,
For it is the only way to—
Fortune for Every Right, Rigorous and Resourceful Individual.

Epilogue

Before I bring the shutters down on this book, I would like to share a nice little verse that touched my heart. It has been written by a colleague, who on reading my first book, *If God Was a Banker* came up to me and pulled out a crumpled paper from the depths of a folder she was carrying. She said she had written this poem a few days into her first job.

Sometimes in my mind, a thought does dwell
How does one live life well
Religion, status, money and fame
Is one taught to play this game?

With scruples to kill, for all that is nice
Does honesty really pay a good price?
Baffled, I'm sure, you may feel
This winding road to get uphill.

Honour and pride are all yesteryear's charms
Now it is one after the other, out to harm
Humanity for sure has taken a turn
I bet, God himself is saying, 'What have I done?'

Each one is out to beat the rest,
With morals and values put to test
How much is true, who is to tell
God's heaven on earth is turning to a hell.

But life is short and its end is certain
It's all in the rise and fall of a curtain
And, when it is time for you to pass
Prepare for the questions that He might ask.

NEOMI LOBO

All through this book, I have spoken of the means required to own the Ferrari, the skill-sets necessary to trudge along on the path to fulfil ones dreams and aspirations.

This poem, however, is a sad commentary on what people actually end up doing in their pursuit of success. And, this is why many fail to achieve the Ferrari.

Engulfed in our desperation and dauntless enthusiasm, to acquire a Ferrari, people often tend to pay no heed to their scruples, conscience, morals, values, honour, pride ... the traits that make a human. The Ten Commandments laid out herein go for a toss. I would like to caution all the aspirants that the Ferrari at the cost of humanity, is not a Ferrari worth fighting for. It is not something which you deserve and it will not stay with you. At some point or the other it will desert you, and you will never again get an opportunity to own one in your entire life.

So folks, as I sign off, I would implore all of you to believe that you have it in you to acquire the Ferrari, despite the fact that in times of cut-throat competition it is not easy to acquire one. If you make an honest effort, it can be yours. There are no shortcuts. Do not even try to find one. Back yourself to get there with integrity and hard work. There will be many detractors along the way, but they are the ones who have attempted to get there and failed. So, do not let them distract you. Keep going. However, there is only one person in this world who can prevent you from getting to the Ferrari ... You, yourself!!

Once your Ferrari arrives ... protect it. Maintain it, give others a ride on it and ... drive carefully. The pride that a Ferrari brings with it is of paramount importance to you and your family. So, keep it intact.

One day, not too long ago, I returned home to find my daughter, Anusha in a very chirpy mood. Normally, by the time I get back home, she is extremely cranky, as it would be very close to her bed time. I could not help talking to her, despite her being tucked into bed and despite the warnings from my mother to let her sleep, as she had to get to school the next morning.

'*Appa*,' she said, 'you know what happened in school today?'

I went into her bedroom and lowered myself on her bed, hugged her, and began patting her to sleep.

'*Appa*,' she continued, 'you know Nishant, the boy who troubles me in school?' I just nodded.

'Prarthana and I got him to say "sorry" today.' She was besides herself with joy. She had told me many times in the past about this bully in her class, who would keep harassing them, but I had not acted on it as I wanted them to learn to deal with bullies.

'How did you manage that?' I asked her, even as I placed my hands over her eyes, getting her to close them, it was but a poor attempt at getting her to sleep.

'I told him that if he doesn't say sorry, my father who's a big author, will write about him in his next book ... and he ran to us, said sorry and disappeared.' I neither reacted nor moved. It took another five minutes for Anusha to slip into her dreamland.

As I made my way out of her room, I could not help but ponder over a simple fact. I was not the only one for whom, my stature, my success, and acquiring the Ferrari was important. It was important for Anusha, too. There are others, too, who want a ride in my Ferrari. If not for myself, I should strive and achieve it for them.

I shut the bedroom door lightly, and walked into the confines of my room, promising myself that after a good night's rest, I would begin tomorrow morning with a new vigour, a new energy, a new passion, and a renewed promise, to make the gleaming **FERRARI** my own.